The Letters

Does anybody truly have no regrets?

Wayne Debernardi

First published by Busybird Publishing 2020

978-1-922465-08-5 (paperback)

978-1-922465-09-2 (ebook)

Cover design: Busybird Publishing

Layout and typesetting: Busybird Publishing

busybird
publishing

Busybird Publishing
2/118 Para Road
Montmorency, Victoria
Australia 3094
www.busybird.com.au

About the Author

Wayne Debernardi was born in Victoria, Australia where he still lives with his wife Lesley and their lovable Labradoodle, Charlie (Charlie Hoover Brown Debernardi). Lesley and Wayne are also blessed with five adult children and their chosen partners and enjoy the many family gatherings, particularly on any given Wednesday night.

With journalism qualifications and a Master of Arts (Writing), Wayne's business and creative writing experience spans four decades. With a passion for writing, Wayne is now pursuing a life-long ambition and turning his creativity into fiction. The Letters is the first of several books on the horizon.

Dedications

For my beloved wife Lesley who had the faith and fortitude to push me to completing a long-desired result; I am eternally grateful.

In loving memory of Sandy.

Driftwood

I am like driftwood,
With as many scars –
Mementos of sand, sea and time,
Soothed and engrained
By experience,
Dreams and false expectation,
Regrets and exaltation,
Love and loss
      Of all that time can offer.

Time is scant,
When it comes to these ideals –
Yet, I have roamed
From shore to shore
And moved with many a tide,
I have dived in and out
      Of hearts and minds,

Now left abandoned
To weather the final storm
Mayhap you come across me,
And see into my dying soul,
You may reach out
        As I reach out to you,

Love me one last time
As I yearn for your love
And your gentle touch,
Take me from this isolation,
Place me upon your mantelpiece –
        And let us warm by your fire

                    WSD

Prologue

Anxiety hits at different times, affects people in different ways.

There can be the gripping of the heart dreading an attack, chills and fevers, deathly silence and screams, even out-of-body experiences. The latter may be scary, but not as scary as the fear of not surviving the experience.

Like most people of his age, he had experienced anxiety at one time or another, but for him, it was still a passing phenomenon. His worst experiences were far behind him. He had experienced the *phenomenon* only once or twice in his lifetime. Even then, they usually related to the stress of advising companies on multi-million dollar deals. Was this his nadir? Perhaps, and if that was the case, he had only experienced something like it a few rare times.

Instead, his life was one of peace and control. Very much one of control.

And yet, this was such unfamiliar territory; the terrain was rough with jagged edges in his mind. He was out of his depth for the first time since - well, he couldn't quite remember when. That invoked a different kind of fear.

God. Should I have believed in God more, he wondered. He smiled wryly at his own parody.

He had learnt much about different religions, having dealt with many cultures over the years, but he had lost his own sense of faith eons ago, it seemed. His trust in Catholicism died for many reasons and at one stage he had considered the simplicity of Hinduism. It was a good fit for many reasons; belief in one god, plus it recognised Adam and Eve, or at least a variation thereof. Actually, that was taking it a bit far, but he had read of Manu and Shatrupa and so arrived at some kind of delusional comparison. Ultimately, he had decided against all religious chicanery.

If he be heaven-meant or hell-bent, the so-called gods would work it out. As a colleague had once said, "You have to believe in hell's existence to go there." He thought he had seen enough of hell over the years, but he also thought the hellish moments had never outweighed the good times. And he had indeed, had some very good times.

He did believe in turning ash to ash, dust to dust. But then again, he liked the Greek mythology concept of the phoenix rising from the ashes. In his mind, a second chance. Next time round he would come back as a cheetah. Sure, he might get shot down by an evil, money-hungry trophy hunter, but at least he would have the advantage of speed to make a decent race of it.

Regardless of his musings, he had no affection for religion, and he suspected one needed some level of passion to believe.

Yet worry about the afterlife – or lack thereof – was not where his anxiousness was rooted. Anxiety, fear, anger, passion and most other emotions come from the decisions you make or choose not to make. That was his belief, without the validation of any religion.

But in reality, it was only three months ago when the pain, short breaths and, sometimes, that unsettling feeling of not being in his own skin started its disturbing journey into his being. That was his personal novena. The wakeup call to pray to whoever and whatever religion or belief system could possibly be listening.

It took several board meetings across a portfolio of companies, where he was president, chairman, director or esteemed past president, to bring things to a head. His comments, especially at one particular recent presiding, came so far out of left field that they were brought into question.

The fact was that some comments - albeit remarks which he would stand solidly by - were not considered in the best interests of the business at hand. They were deemed irrelevant.

In his own thinking, his comments, while not considered complimentary to a board of fuckwits who had no other interest other than collecting their quarterly dispensary, were more than adequate.

He thought back to one encounter where he had openly said, "You may not think my comment relevant, but do the sums just once, and you will find the company seven million dollars better off, compared with last year."

The directors who had voted him down were made to eat humble pie and everything could have been left alone, except he'd told them to: "Hand in your resignations along with your balls and for those without, your clitoris." Another clearly minuted meeting to regret.

But he knew the audit to be falsified. He had a strong background in such matters. He also knew his target was a corrupt chief executive officer, who would need to forge a career anywhere else, anytime, preferably immediately.

***

Stopping the past reflections and coming to grips with the people around him, he forced himself to focus and come back to the present. Pulse taken. Equipment shuffled into place. Hushed tones offering calm platitudes with no purpose.

It was all happening around him and for a man always in control, firmly at the helm, there was nothing he could do. He felt completely out of sorts – a new experience and like being out of sorts, not one he was comfortable with.

In his heyday, a simple wave of a hand, a finger pointed, a smile or grimace gave his directions, and all would be done without question. Now, the tables had definitely turned.

He laid back; the bright lights tilted so as not to totally

blind him and yet, he felt like a 'roo caught in fast, onrushing headlights'.

He had made commercial decisions. Personal decisions. Final decisions that tempted fate or, at the very least, brought impending fate to his door.

Then many images passed his mind, ever so rapidly.

Faces and names seemed to float in circles within the bright lights.

He was both a scholar and an educator. There were meetings with presidents and despots. He had led business conquests, written books, helped to develop communities, and now a smile came through his pursed lips.

He had loved beautiful women and been, at times, loved by them. And now a bright light, what did it all mean?

What had Vincent said to him? "You are making a big mistake; you'll be back bigger and better, so why close down?"

"Just in case someone else thinks they can make a decision without me in my absence," was his reply.

"Besides, Vincent," he added, "I'm tired of being on top of the deck; time I reshuffled the deck and did something different."

Suddenly, with all of these thoughts, a deep breath and all anxiety seemed to peel away. Contentment is a strange feeling, but that was how he felt at that moment.

Now, the count-down. Ten, nine, eight, seven.... blessed sleep and sweet dreams.

Part One

Reacquainting *Emily*

I measure every grief I meet
With narrow, probing, eyes –
I wonder if it weighs like mine –
Or has an easier size
I measure every grief I meet

Emily Dickinson

Chapter One

Eyelashes. Interesting devices of the human body. They flutter to avoid dust. They express emotion, quicker than any other part of the body. They dip to hide shame and fear. They celebrate intention and fan lust.

Right now, the eyelashes of one Desmond Jamieson were brushing his skin, not wanting his eyelid muscles to move but then, reluctantly, those muscles pushed his lashes upward and what seemed to be so heavy began to move.

First, at slow camera shutter-speed. Then a blink and then another. The blur slowly resided. He was awake. His throat parched, utter nausea wracking his body.

But he was awake. That was a relief in itself.

He closed his eyes to the dazzling white light which had decided to bounce off the sterile and equally white walls like a ping pong ball off a bat at high speed.

Closed eyes helped stem the nausea but not the reality, so he gradually allowed them to open again. One eye at a time, slowly. Very slowly.

He moved, ever so gradually, attempting to take in his surrounds but this also proved difficult. No, actually painful. Very, very painful. The tubes stemming in and out of his body pulled sharply, adding to his discomfort and nausea.

A female voice sounded from somewhere in the room. A nurse at the foot of his bed spoke softly, warning him to not make sudden moves.

Geez, now you tell me.

"Just lay still, Mr Jamieson," she said. Still on his side, he looked towards the direction of the voice, finally able to see an upper portion of the nurse scribing something on a chart, clipping it back into place at the end of the bed.

"So what's the verdict?" he asked, grimacing. Talking was also painful, as if every syllable was being yanked out of his head, one tooth at a time.

His question, however, was flatly stated as if in a rehearsal. His voice was devoid of quaver or feeling of his current pain. His question was suddenly irrelevant, fearing an answer that was inevitable.

"Mr Chan will be in to see you soon."

At that, he shut his eyes momentarily. The eyelashes performed their duty. He knew what it meant.

There was nothing left to be done. Of course, while he had tried to remain positive, even chirpy, leading up to the operation, his worst fears had now been realised, with a simple, *"Mr Chan will be in to see you soon."*

And indeed Mr Chan was soon there in front of him, maybe a half hour after the nurse had left. He was well acquainted with Mr Chan, or Leon, as he had come to know him.

Leon Chan stood five foot nothing. His face was as creased as a rumpled, unironed shirt, and yet, in complete contrast, he bore a bald head as smooth as a baby's bottom.

Not that Jamieson had anything against a bald head. He had only just started to regrow his own hair, following the last bout of chemotherapy a little more than twelve months prior. It was now at a sharp bristle and it amazed him that it was darker than the salt and pepper beard he had. The beard was cropped short, neatly following his facial contours to the new growth on his scalp.

He had been very specific with Shelley at the barber shop he frequented. Shelley definitely had talent but he wondered who actually did her hair. Bright, rusty red with a huge streak of purple; simply, Desmond couldn't quite get the colour combination. Then again, he never understood the nose ring and the number of tattoos she, and others of her age for that matter, chose to inflict upon their bodies.

"No probs, Dezzo, you're in good hands," Shelley chirped. And indeed he was. She had completed the task to perfection.

Now his precisely trimmed beard and slightly bristled hair was before the gaze of the wonder surgeon, Mr Leon Chan.

When they first met, Desmond had thought Chan may have come straight out of a P.T. Barnum circus but was soon to realise that even the adored Phileas Barnum could not have had the magic touch of such an excellent and renowned surgeon.

Mr Leon Chan had already saved Desmond's life. But salvage comes with no guarantees and a few months later; the remorseless cancer took a different direction.

Desmond had always referred to his surgeon as Doc or Leon, but in reality, he was always a Mr.

Desmond never had a lot of time for titles, regardless of his own business status. He had once given a lecture to a university of would-be business graduates and made a very clear point of saying, "If you are going in to make millions or make a name or title of yourself, you might, *just might,* become a leader; or equally, you may become nothing more than a sheep amongst an immensely competitive flock."

Leon Chan, whilst normally impersonal in the way he spoke to his patients, sat gently on the edge of Jamieson's bed.

In normal cases he would be apologetic but curt, as he felt it helped the patient *get to the point.* There was no benefit to sugar-coating medical facts.

Before Chan started to speak, the patient feebly raised his hand and said, "It's okay."

"Desmond, my... can I call you a friend and not just a patient?" asked Chan.

Desmond nodded.

"I know we both knew of the probabilities but until we operated, regardless of the scans, we didn't know how much damage, or how far-spreading, the cancer was," Chan said.

The cancer had spread into other areas of his stomach, the lining of his intestine was eroding, and his pancreas would soon be under threat.

Desmond just asked one question; "How long?"

At that point - and he had never done so with any other patient - Leon Chan took the hand of Desmond Jamieson.

"We have formed a bond over our time," said the surgeon.

"It's okay; how long?" repeated Desmond.

"The time you have is up to you, to a certain extent. You can choose to go into an induced coma, or you can choose to sit it out a little longer. I can't make that decision for you, but I must warn you, Desmond, that decision may come with growing, and at times, very sharp pain. Morphine is going to be a very good friend," said Leon.

Desmond Jamieson, at the age of sixty-eight, would ultimately be going into palliative care, and await the meeting with his maker, if in fact, the maker existed. There were times over the preceding months he had hoped there would be a God, or at least somewhere nice that he could live a life of solace. He would soon return as a cheetah, after all.

He imagined scenes of clear streams and lush grass, and perhaps a fishing rod, its line dangling with the odd bob in the water signalling a fine catch. He didn't give a damn if there was a fish nibbling at the bait; they were fed, and he was relaxed on a riverbank. Perhaps a place where he could catch up on all the books he never got to read, just like the movies he always said he would hire from the DVD shop but never did.

He loved old westerns in particular.

Henry Fonda at his best, John Wayne with his rip-roaring voice, and Jimmy Stewart, with a purposeful drawl, particularly in that film with Lee Marvin – gee, what was it – the Man who Shot Liberty Valance, yes, that was it. That was a John Wayne movie, but the other stars grabbed the limelight. It was only one of a couple that Des recalled in which John

Wayne died but in this case, only by reference; the film never showed him dying, not like in *The Alamo* or *The Cowboys*.

He was very much a fan of Eastwood, all the way through the spaghetti western phase and through to eternity. Having recently seen Pale Rider again, Des was a happy man.

He was still hanging on to the visual and realised his mind had drifted while Mr Chan explained the next steps, the month or few weeks he may have left. Desmond Jamieson was not really paying that much attention, but he gave the courtesy of pretending to listen. The surgeon's words seemed to be washing over him.

"Thank you Leon. I know you have done your best. I think I might just wait it out for a little while before I ring upstairs to see if there is a vacancy," said Desmond, his eyes looking upward to the ceiling.

I told you Vincent, double or nothing; aren't you regretting not taking up the bet?

A carer would be appointed to his ward which was on the other side of the hospital. He did hear that.

Of course the ward may not be his final room before eternity dawned. It would be a weighing station, a stop-over, a place before another place when he could no longer stand or think for himself.

A ward, far away from those who would live well beyond the here and now, Des thought to himself.

He closed his eyes again, to shut out a single tear but he didn't know exactly what was upsetting him. He had known, deep down in his soul, this was the way it was going to end.

He had consented to entry to the ResiCare hostel regardless of Vincent's challenges but in reality, deep-down, Desmond always knew of the inevitability of death. His gut instinct that had served him so well for decades was, most unfortunately, still mercilessly accurate.

Vincent, to his credit, knew of the mastery of Jamieson, his ability to manage the most ridiculous of outcomes. Vincent had also challenged Desmond to a ridiculous bet of three hundred thousand dollars on his survival. A bet that they would later share some mirth over, but never any actual exchange of currency.

Vincent had questioned his choice. "Let's wait and see Desmond, let's wait and see." But he had told Vincent to prepare for the worst and then celebrate the victory if in fact, the worst was defeated.

But Desmond had made a clear decision that if the news was not in his favour, then it would be in no one's favour, personally or from a business perspective.

The decision to go into hostel mode was an uneasy one. He had to have a lot of his personal things placed in storage, but again, Vincent would cater for this just as Vincent had catered for so many things in Jamieson's life over the past few decades.

A key factor in Des' decision was there were so few to worry about him, regardless of all he did or had done. Most importantly, he did not want to die alone in any of his houses or apartments.

Of course, beyond the hostel which, all in all, was only temporary accommodation, he would have to face those final stages of life in palliative care. Something he was not yet ready to contemplate.

He had deliberated for weeks but realised it would be best for all concerned that his affairs were in order and that his business interests and holdings were in a healthy position to continue in his absence. His decision had been partly made in memory of those before him who had not organised their lives as well as he had.

Now, the reality was coming home. His absence this time would be one from which there would be no return.

Vincent had said he was becoming Murphy-like. Jamieson said that he was wrong; that according to O'Neill's Law, Murphy was an optimist. Vincent conceded and they had both laughed.

Now, there were sudden thoughts and faces flooding

through his weary mind, of so many people, some already departed, others he was not so sure about. Their very existence had escaped him. Time had escaped him.

His tear, and he knew there would be other tears, was about the inevitability of it all. The inevitability of mortality.

"I could not stop for death, so he kindly stopped for me."

Emily Dickinson's words came rushing in. He did not understand how his mind could cite such works after all of these years. Images and words enveloped him, smothering him to such an extent that the nausea overcame him, causing him to vomit, which inflicted its own torture as the catheters pulled hard on both sides of his lower body.

"The carriage held but just ourselves, and immortality."

Of course, vomiting is easy until there is nothing there to vomit and so dry retching followed until pure bile spilled through his lips. The mustard-yellow liquid drooled, then continued with another wave, and another, wracking his body with pain at every convulsion.

Mr Chan called for the nurse to wipe away the fluid from his craggy-lined mouth. Then the surgeon shook Jamieson's hand and left without another word, his head bowed.

The nurse just looked, a little sympathetically, but then left just as the good doctor had.

Desmond Jamieson was alone, and that reality was a sudden slap. No, a right hook to his jaw, so hard he imagined hitting the canvas and bouncing. Rocky 1 to 7 or however many sequels there were. He had lived on and off with companionship for all his life; he was comfortable in his own skin, but this was different.

This was the first time he had felt lonely for decades. A sense of reality, permanency, suddenly filled the void.

So this is it, Des, he thought. His second wife had said he would die a lonely old man. She won that bet. Of course, he wasn't *that* old – sixty-eight is hardly old.

Fuck, what have I done with my life?

The nausea lifted again, and he started to dry retch just as the nurse returned. His head thumping, his body resonated with pain as he heaved.

Fuck, is my head caving in as well? Bet she thinks I'm a right bastard too.

But the nurse did her job, lifting his head and placed the bowl under his chin until this last wave of total nausea subsided, the yellowish liquid dribbling into the receptacle.

"I'm going to get the floor doctor," she said.

"Really, is the floor sick too?" Jamieson replied, a feeble attempt at humour, managing a weak smile.

"I think you may be having trouble with the morphine," she replied, denying the mirth of his quick wit. *Unbelievable,* she thought. *Poor bugger.*

A few minutes later she returned with a young man in a white coat. Des looked up without a murmur, thinking how very young they are. Perhaps at that moment, he was an old man after all.

This 'kid' looked just that, a kid. But he must have done his time, the eight years plus they required to be here in the first place. Funny, Des thought suddenly, his apprenticeship was much more of hard knocks and yet this kid was going to make it all right, even for a moment or two.

"Considering there was only exploratory surgery done and that we have you on morphine for the pain, I think we may get you off that," the child doctor announced.

"Fine," responded Jamieson, "I'd rather not be heaving all over the sick floor." While that got a quizzical look from the doctor, the nurse certainly gave a light chuckle.

"Just the same," said the child doctor, "We will need to dose you up pretty high on pethidine to help with the pain."

Weariness started to succumb.

"We slowly drove, he knew no haste, and I had put away my labour, and my leisure too, for his civility."

Desmond Jamieson saw a gaunt female, clad in a white linen dress. She gently swayed back and forth, whispering,
"Parting is all we know of heaven and all we need of hell."
His eyes gradually closed. This time, both doctor and nurse were still in the room.

Chapter Two

Lauren Black read the charts, well skilled in doing so after the past eight years. Here she was, in her grey skirt and vibrant magenta blouse. Colour in her perspective counted.

Another life chapter to be concluded here, within the boundaries of these walls.

These walls, of course, would change from the private hostel quarters to the less appealing but still private quarters of palliative care known in the hospital as PalCare. Her job was to be part of that journey, a mere crossing of corridors and hallways.

The thought was brief and customary. She recognised inevitability more than most people would in their lifetime. No. All their lifetimes.

She also knew that some of her acquaintances thought her job was nigh on as macabre as any job could be. They did debate whether the job was any different, better or worse than that of an undertaker.

Her closest friends, however, held nothing more than admiration; if not, they held her in some false sense of awe. Then again, she could count her closest friends on less than one hand, if not two fingers. The question remained, out of friends, did majority count?

Undertakers, in her mind, however, were a breed of their own and a breed she respected. After all, they actually dealt with life, helping those left behind, far more than dealing with death.

Her job was somewhat tougher. Her psychology PhD didn't always count and sometimes she wondered if she wouldn't be better off counselling other sick souls, rather than those souls soon to leave this world.

When it came to *soul-talk* as she described it, there were too many discussions where she had to *comply* and understand the individual's need, love and at sometimes hate for their own existence. So often it was a time of immense confusion, depending on their mental frame of mind.

The most placid could become filled with aggression; the outspoken often became sullen; the religious sometimes gave up believing and the non-believers cried out for forgiveness from God.

She thought herself to be an atheist but wanted to think there was something else more worthwhile. So many of her clients needed that reassurance at the end.

She smiled to think of the occasions, more than once, when a Catholic priest had given last rites to an undeclared Jewish person. The parents were horrified of course, but no more so when a rabbi spoke at the head of one bed and recited the Vidui for someone who had never reached out to a church of any kind; not even a shared olive branch.

Of course, she was not always present; in fact, most had left her charge and moved to those final steps of PalCare – some in induced coma state; others soon after. There were seldom final rites served.

But what good does religion do if you do not believe? Her thoughts always remained on the disappointment of religion; the endless discrimination, the endless wars and the violence that religion seemed to take some kind of intrinsic pride in.

Her thoughts turned to a stirring patient, a new client on the block.

The case files for the person in front of her, however, were somewhat scant.

She was also used to that, having to do her own research from time to time, more so when there was no family present to fill in gaps.

The file included all the *vitals.* There was a name, current address and a mobile number for immediate contact with a name -'Vincent' scribbled beside it. His medical condition complemented those notes on the bed chart. *Terminal.*

Other notes read, "We *know who he is, seemingly no real connection to family. No greater level of information from the patient. He appears that he has full insurance coverage for his needs."*

She then noted what was written in the special comments column. *"Take care of this patient; a major supporter of this facility,"* was scribed. Signed off with the initials of AS.

AS. She tried to guess who that may be. *"A major supporter of this facility."* It didn't ring a bell but *AS* was now firmly stuck in her mind.

She sat there waiting for Des Jamieson to awaken. She knew he would be anxious about his new surroundings. It was always an interesting factor, even if they knew of the consequences of time and place.

She would provide an overview of his surroundings, his final weeks ahead. As hospice-palliative case-manager, she had done this some twenty-six times in the past six years.

She knew if the patient denied the outcome, it was hard work. She thought of Jim Trevallis. He denied the inevitability. He refused death until the last, never communicating more than two words in any conversation she had with him.

She remained troubled about Jim, unsure she had done enough to make him as peaceful with the outcome as she had wanted to. Her training was of one to make a difference; she knew deep down, she couldn't have done any better.

Sometimes, it didn't work out and that was a threat to her own sanity, but she exercised belief in herself and her patients concurrently. Jim's demise was not one of those bright or pivotal moments in life, not in her life, anyway.

When she put her head on a pillow at night, she came to grips with the very real fact that her job was to work with people in their final stage of life.

This new patient was lying there, and she hoped his journey would be different. Less painful. And not like Jim Trevallis'.

She considered her position. She was good at her job. She constantly fumbled to describe that satisfaction to anyone.

In that inability for people to accept the role she played, she felt lonely too, not just for her patients.

Damn. I'm nearly 40 years of age. I need to dance. I need to party.

Chapter Three

Des Jamieson didn't just stir from a deep slumber, his body bolted as if lightning had struck. The pain that came with the jolt up into mid-air also brought him back to earth just as quick, back to the confines of white sheets and sterile surroundings.

The dream had surfaced, incomplete and unwelcomed. Before he could get a train of thought, he was looking up with still bleary eyes, at a very attractive, young woman.

Her smile was calming enough, and it was complemented with a, "Just settle back, Mr Jamieson, you're in good hands." However, his focus on the young woman moved beyond the smile. He felt he was still in dream.

"Where am -" he muttered almost inaudibly, stopping abruptly.

"You are in good hands, Mr Jamieson, in the best hands that City General's transition quarters have to offer," she said.

"Really," he said gruffly, "so who are you?"

His eyes still transfixed, realising the drugs, whatever they were, must be having their due effect.

"My name is Lauren, see on my badge, Lauren, Lauren Black," she said in a purposeful and deliberate manner. She knew he may be still coming out of a dream extended by the change in medication which they had introduced during his sleep.

"Lauren. Lauren's a nice name," he stumbled with his words, transfixed upon the young woman's face.

"Thank you."

He momentarily moved his gaze from this young beauty before him, a beauty he had not seen for a very long time.

Lauren was tall and slender in a most elegant and very business-like way. Her magenta-shaded blouse hugged her fine features, while her grey skirt equally followed the contours of a very fit and healthy figure. She had high cheek-bones, a petite nose and light emerald eyes that would make all of Ireland proud; they simply sparkled and smiled with character.

He then chose to take in the broader landscape, his eyes searching the small room. There was a window, with what appeared to be, beyond the curtains, some greenery; perhaps a garden. And there was a door leading out adjacent to that window.

There was no longer a bright, white light and the walls had been magically replaced by the palest of egg-shell blue.

On the other side of the room, there was another door. An ensuite, perhaps. And then there was a door that led to what he considered had to be the rest of the hostel.

After the visual roaming of his confine, Des Jamieson's pale-blue, almost steely-grey eyes met again with those of Lauren Black and he thought, the Irish eyes were indeed smiling.

***

Lauren knew her script. Understand their needs, give them an opening. An opening that would amass fears and acclamations; time given and time lost.

She had watched his gaze and then searching eyes. Those eyes could have equally belonged to a first-time criminal looking for an escape. Indeed, in her experience, many would have wished a far greater escape.

She waited for the inevitable question of "Where am I?" which she assumed was coming when he first awoke. To her surprise, her patient responded somewhat indifferently. Instead his eyes again darted around the room, taking in his new living quarters.

"So, we are in the south wing of the Gerry Hampson building," said Des. Not a question, but a statement.

"Yes, but how did you know?" said Lauren.

Jamieson did not respond, but rather gazed again around the room again and then darted back to meet her eyes. With that, she decided she should push on with induction.

"Again, I'm Lauren and yes, you are right about where you are," she said, blushing because her patient already knew that.

She caught herself in doing so. *Keep it flowing, Lorrie, keep it flowing.*

"You know, and I know," she started, with that inevitable tremble she felt inside absolutely every time. She took a deep breath to steady herself.

"You are dying, and it is my job to make your final journey as comfortable and meaningful as I possibly can."

Jamieson considered her words carefully. As she spoke, he considered the words to be rehearsed, yet eloquent and precise.

Eloquent and precise. Not sure that's how he had imagined it, but there it was - *Eloquent and precise.*

"So, Miss Black, what exactly do you consider to be comfortable and meaningful?" he asked in a matter-of-fact fashion.

Her further blushing told him he had caught her off guard with his direct question, but she rose to the occasion. She had expected the normal dramatic pause or trembling reality.

Yet, she also knew from looking at the monitor, understanding the high pethidine ration, this was a man fighting for his time to understand - also, the fight against fatigue, which was kicking in, big time.

"Comfortable is with as little pain as possible," she replied, knowing this to be an increasingly impossible feat as time went by.

"Meaningful, is to help you fulfil your days with any last wishes that help you have peace of mind."

"I see," he pondered, adding, "So, Miss Black, you will take me away from here so we can go fishing?"

"Mr Jamieson, please call me Lauren. And no, you know I am not taking you fishing."

With a very brief smile, he replied, "Yes, I do know. And please call me Des."

He looked again, directly into Lauren Black's eyes. A very faint memory, perhaps. There was something special about this well-rehearsed woman; something for the memory bank whilst he could still hold onto it.

"The carriage held but just ourselves."

He closed his eyes just for a second to savour whatever that memory may have given a glimpse of. It came up empty; perhaps, just a wish for recollection and he suddenly wondered if this was the beginning of the end of both sweet and sour memories.

When his eyes took on those of his allocated new carer before him, he saw a young woman doing what he thought to be a most difficult job; putting up with arseholes like him. Those deep-pooled, yet pale green eyes of Ms Black got a gaze of admiration.

"So," she began to speak again but was interrupted once more.

"So, let's start with the comfort stakes, shall we?"

"What do you mean?"

"Get rid of all these damn tubes," he said. "I am most capable of walking over to that ensuite, brushing my teeth, even having a shower, who knows, perhaps even walking out to that garden past that door".

"I know that's how you feel now but..."

Again, he interrupted.

"Yes I know about the but, but but is not now – let's wait

until but time kicks in, or when it indeed kicks me in the butt," he said adamantly.

"OK," Lauren conceded softly. "But it can't happen for a day or two. There are still blood tests and ensuring we have you on the right strength pain killers."

"Right." Desmond started but it was her time to interrupt.

"And regardless, Mr Jamieson..."

"Des."

"Des, you need to have the drip in all of the time. I can't have you here in pain when it can be avoided," she finally finished.

"OK, understood," he replied with a sigh, giving in to her assertiveness.

"We need to keep up some heavy dosage of pethidine, considering your nauseous reaction to the morphine. So, the drip will need to remain but if the nursing staff are OK with it, you can walk with it and it can be tapped for you to have a shower if that is your desire. But there will come a time when that won't work, and I need you to be aware."

"Understood."

This time it was her turn to look into her patient's eyes. She did so with a flicker of admiration, acknowledging his stance for his own dignity.

"You will be drowsy; you will need plenty of rest."

"Yes." He was already feeling weary.

"It's eleven o'clock. I'm sure we can have you unplugged and hopefully unwired by tomorrow afternoon."

"Thanks."

"I have to do some other work right now, but I will be back to see you this afternoon, if that's alright with you."

"Sure. I'm not going anywhere," he responded with a slight grin.

"In the meantime, I want you to think of anyone you need to see – your wife, your family, your friends – anybody you want me to contact."

"I think I may have a little rest now and see you this afternoon," he said, evading what she had just said.

Lauren Black left the room wondering if he had actually heard her or just chose to dismiss the thought of outside contact. Perhaps, she would know in the afternoon.

But Jamieson did hear Lauren's words. He closed his eyes and started to think and saw a myriad of people floating in his mind. Some he genuinely considered he should talk to; others were ghosts he was unsure of the need to reacquaint with or in fact, whether they needed to be woken at all.

Chapter Four

Desmond Jamieson had indeed heard the parting words of Lauren Black. He didn't just choose to ignore them; there was something more paramount. The words actually scared him.

I want you to think of anyone you need to see – your wife, your family, your friends – anybody you want me to contact.

Christ, he thought – do I really need this? He had already packed up most of his belongings, tidied up most of his business affairs, had drafted his last will and testament; he just had to sign the documents that Vincent would dutifully deliver. Even if he keeled over now, he wouldn't die intestate, even if he wanted to tweak beneficiaries.

Carol would be looked after until her final breath and there was no point in seeing or talking to her. She was beyond any comprehension – had been for seventeen months. He had gone to see her for the last time only a week ago.

Carol had been a doting wife, his third and final, for the past nine years. She had put up with his distant travels away and late-night business meetings and through it all still managed to be by his side at every important occasion.

Some of the media had painted an ugly picture or at least, ugly in his mind. Carol had all the looks of an ageing beauty queen and the editorial had suggested she was a trophy wife and a possible gold digger. Desmond had been furious and with a single phone call, a retraction was made along with an apology but as media goes, all too late. Even then, he was philosophical. As the old saying goes, *'Today's news, tomorrow's fish and chip wrappings.'* It was the principle of the thing.

There was no doubt that Carol enjoyed being in the limelight afforded by Desmond's business dealings and social circles, but she did love him, regardless of their nineteen year age difference. However, Carol also had two vices. She smoked non-stop and she loved to party and party hard.

Regardless of his constant plea for Carol to slow down, she continued at a frantic pace. He had been oblivious to her delving into various pills atop of her addition to the chain smoking and alcohol, so when she had a stroke at the age of forty-six, he was more than shocked; he was mortified.

He blamed himself and cursed his work which habitually took him away from the importance of their relationship. As he thought of it now, he cursed himself even further; after all, was that not his whole life over? She had been found a few hours post-incident and the brain had been starved too long – she was paralysed down one side and was deemed to be in a vegetative state.

So cross Carol off the contact list. She had been a true mate and he missed her badly. She had come into his life several years after his marriage to Vivian collapsed, both tumultuously and expensively. The years between were consumed with his work and a series of brief affairs, none that could ever be considered as meaningful as the bond he had formed with Carol. Yes, he missed her badly.

His parents had long passed, not that it mattered. He had *divorced* them when he was eighteen years old and in fact, his mother some time earlier.

His mother, Marianne, had been an alcoholic for most of his childhood and by the end was mixing drugs and gin as fast as anyone in living history. Of course that history was short-lived, and she died at the age of forty-eight (a bad precursor to being married to Carol, who would most likely die at a similar age) from the toxins and the abuse hand-delivered by his father, Allen.

Allen had always been short-tempered but decided to take his anguish out on the young Des, more so, after Marianne's passing.

Desmond did his best to look after his younger sister, Lee, during those early, tumultuous years. Four years his junior, Lee had been a vibrant child, full of life but that life was cut short as well. Lee had been crossing a road at the corner shop and was hit by a car.

They kept Lee alive in a coma for almost two months and then her small body just gave in. That night his father had too much to drink which was no different than the norm and decided to throw a fist at Desmond, but by then he was not only taller and stronger, he had been in training, boxing at the local gym.

Allen Jamieson was admitted to hospital after two very quick swings of Desmond's fists. The police had been called in by neighbours reporting yet another disturbance of the peace. They cautioned the youth, but he had already made up his mind.

He was getting out and heading for the city. He had saved enough money to tide him over at a hostel and had his application in for numerous city jobs.

He had just finished high school and was waiting for his final results. He had spoken to the local postmaster, Mr Matthews, whom he knew well and promised as soon as he had some form of fixed abode, he would call with a forwarding address. He had built a strong friendship over the years with the postmaster, having helped out at the post office and mowing the Matthews' lawns after school. Mr Matthews was not a rich man but well placed in the town community and he always paid an extra fiver to Desmond over the agreed amount.

When Desmond called Mr Matthews a week later from a hostel in Carlton just a few kilometres from the heart of the city, the postmaster had informed him of mail which he would dutifully forward to Desmond.

In high anticipation, it was indeed his high school examination results which, when they arrived in the mail, were quite staggering, well beyond even young Desmond's expectations. His hopes were realised; the results placed him in the highest bracket in the State and would be sure to hold him in good stead with prospective employers.

Twelve months later, Desmond Jamieson was firmly ensconced in his first job as an accounts clerk with one of the 'Big Four' financial firms. He had a salary which afforded him rental at a modest apartment in Carlton, within a short tram ride to work and to the university where he had enrolled for his tertiary accounting studies.

Things were looking up for the very first time in his life. Then he got the call from Mr Matthews, who regretted to advise Desmond of his father's passing.

Chapter Five

Some of the stories that came to be connected with the passing of Allen Jamieson were fanciful to say the least, or that was how they struck his son, Desmond.

One such tale had Allen in a pub brawl, beating half of his rivals before falling and hitting his head. This particular version could have been true, but Des was unconvinced about the numbers involved.

Another story had the deceased cheating at cards and having the living daylights thrashed out of him. Des thought this a definite possibility until he learned of the gun wound.

The fate of Allen Jamieson came to pass when he had decided to break into a house a mere block away from his family home. He had thought it vacant until he tripped over a vase in the hallway of the said residence, awakening its owner, an off-duty police officer. The rest was history; the gun was fired, and Allen died within seconds.

Desmond arranged the funeral out of some misguided sense of responsibility. It was there he planned for his father to be buried next to his mother and his sister, Lee, in the Hastings cemetery but it was also when he was reintroduced to his aunt, Charlotte.

Charlotte was a short, stubby woman with bulging flabs hanging from every angle of her body, making her look as round as she was tall, and she was the only living relative of both Allen and Desmond Jamieson.

Des had deliberately planned not to say anything at the service; he had simply nothing to say. He just wanted the whole process and the day to be over and done with. After all, he had arranged a decent burial service but deep down he could not find a single kind word to say about the departed. Charlotte had her own predetermined attitude to life.

Charlotte had been driven to the service by a so-called friend, Ethel, who was gaunt to say the least. Skeletal would be a more appropriate for Ethel, who was appropriately dressed in funeral black in a Mortisha Addams fashion. She didn't carry beheaded roses, but long sleeves cover many mysteries and scars.

Charlotte, hair dyed in a somewhat putrid, strawberry-blonde, had gotten out of the car in the muddy, grassed area in front of the church, taking a final swig of a bottle in a brown paper bag and then throwing it into the back of the car.

Des had greeted his Aunt with a simple, "Hello and nice to see you, Auntie Charlotte."

The response was a curt and more pointed, "Fuck you."

The service was to be a simple affair and in fact there were no more than twenty people who sat in the church pews that day. In Desmond's mind, it spoke volumes and yet, he still thought he was 'doing the right thing'.

Not only did Charlotte, amidst the simple service, break into the most pretentious and dismal outcry of loss for her dear brother, she went on a rampage against Desmond.

"You are nothing but a cur to this family; a whelping good for nothing," she shrilled at the top of a quavering voice.

The priest, Father Greg, shook his head in dismay and then continued his sermon.

"You up and left when your family needed you the most. Your father was cryin' out for you and where the fuck woz you?"

"You can hide in your tailored suit, but you killed your father, my poor, fuckin', innocent brother," she cried.

The priest took a deep breath and continued in solemn

tones. Desmond thought it was perhaps Latin, although it may have been a little rusty.

The two policemen regulated to be there also shook their heads. There had been conceived ideas of family or friends taking umbrage towards the police; after all, it was a police officer who had duly ended the life of Allen Jamieson. Of course that was all folly. There was only shrill Charlotte, and Allen had next to no friends to mention.

Des was more than quizzical at their presence, wondering who actually cared.

With Charlotte's rants, Desmond merely closed his eyes and shook his head, saddened the so-called family had come down to this. He thought of his beloved sister, Lee and hoped she had found a better place than this debacle.

Then came a moment of truth. Father Greg asked Desmond to come to the pulpit to speak of his father. No-one that had been approached by the priest or funeral director had offered to speak, including the beloved sister of the deceased, Charlotte.

Desmond slowly rose and made his way to the lectern. He had not prepared a speech but in his mind, it was time to settle some truths and seal some open wounds.

Even as he made his way, there was yet another jibe from the more than half-drunken Charlotte.

"Just have a look at this dandy boy in his fine suit," she sneered. Ethel aka Mortisha, was clinging to Clara's arm, not to discourage her friend but to support the outrage. To egg her on.

Desmond thought of the irony of having to lay-by this off-the-rack suit from Fletcher Jones, his first real suit that cost two-hundred and fifty dollars and took three months for him to pay off. A suit personally tailored for him was in another league back then.

The thought process and the constant abhorrent screams from his aunt, along with his almost primitive reaction to his father's passing suddenly consumed him.

"We are," he started, almost trembling, "here to celebrate, no scratch that, to recognise the life and time of my father, Allen Jamieson.

"I don't know many of you and for those I recognise, I'm not sure of your feelings, or devotion, if any, to my father."

Suddenly, Desmond was feeling stronger, his voice unfaltering.

"If you had any true relationship with my father, please raise your hand and feel free to share your story," he said and momentarily paused.

There was no hand-raising and even Charlotte momentarily fell quiet.

"My father," Desmond continued, "had a hard life," Charlotte nodded fervently. "but his life, in my opinion, was not only short lived but so self-indulgent, he warrants little of our time, other than to pray for his soul and say goodbye.

"He was a bully, an abuser, a drunk and while it saddens me on this solemn occasion to say and more so, within these hallowed walls, a true bastard."

There was murmur and another muted groan in Latin from Father Greg.

And then it happened. Charlotte's wrath reenergised.

"How fucking dare you say that about your own father? My brother," she cried out.

"And where were you, Charlotte, for all of those years?" asked Desmond.

The semi-drunk or half-doped Charlotte, Desmond wasn't sure which, ignored the question.

"You couldn't even look after that dumb sister of yours. What was her name, Loretta?" she spat out.

That was enough. The last straw.

Desmond quietly left his place at the pulpit, walked calmly up to his aunt and whispered in her ear, "Her name was Lee, and you will go to fucking hell, you stupid bitch."

He turned to leave, facing the congregation of some twenty people; several who had merely come in from the cold and most of whom were waiting for the church soup kitchen to spark warmth in their hungry bellies and troubled souls.

Others were merely busybodies and gossip-mongers. In his mind and at that time, the event was a reflection of old folklore with dragons breathing in all of the poisons and breathing out flames of purity, and he was suddenly light-headed and dizzy. He had just drawn a line under his childhood, by simply saying goodbye to his father.

So scratch all next of kin from Ms Black's list.

Part Two

A Kestrel for a Knave

"It's fierce, an' it's wild, an' it's not bothered about anybody, not even about me, right. And that's why it's so great."

Barry Hines, A Kestrel for a Knave.

Chapter Six

Lying in his hospital bed, drowsy and a little uncomfortable, Desmond started to reminisce; a chapter of his life that he had tried hard not to revisit or at least not revisit too often.

Desmond had returned to work immediately following the travesty of his father's funeral. He felt no remorse and wondered if that was healthy but soon dismissed any attempt to analyse the situation further.

He had a career to forge and that was his only intent. He studied at night, worked in the office by day, and attempted to get sleep and exercise when it was possible to do so.

The first five years on the job seemed to fly by and early promotion was on the cards; all was looking up for Desmond. Then he met Karen Swanson, or Kes, as she was introduced by a colleague who knew her well. He had not seen a more beautiful woman in all his life.

Kes was tall and as graceful as the swan in her name. Her wavy brown hair, high cheekbones, slender nose and pale green eyes captivated him instantly; not to mention the most beautiful hour-glass figure he had ever seen.

Kes had been appointed to the firm and like Des, she was a hard worker and studying even harder than he was. He was working towards his first degree but Kes had the brains to go for a double major and a Bachelor of Commerce to boot. To Des, that was simply impressive.

There was always small talk between them. *What did you get up to on the weekend? Isn't the weather crap?* Not much more and Des remained quiet as the feelings stirred within him; a growing and unanswered passion.

Of course, he had dated girls during his high school years, with mixed results; some happy times, some experiences on the verge of disaster. Amidst the two extremes was Felicity, to whom he gave up his virginity at the age of sixteen. He had been feeling cavalier one night and asked if he could walk her home from a party.

Des was the chivalrous one while Felicity had other things in mind. She was twelve months older than Des and while crossing a flood-lit football oval on the way to her house, she taunted Des.

Taking her t-shirt off and then her bra, followed by her long flowing, linen skirt, she lay down on the oval turf, making her intentions clear.

"Well, I've taken my gear off, mostly – are you man enough to take off the rest?" she said.

The rest was history and after that encounter they never dated or spoke to each other again.

Twelve months passed since meeting Kes, and for Des they passed slowly. He often saw Kes getting into a car of an evening; the boyfriend picking her up to take her home. Des' envy had to be kept in check.

He went out with a few girls; one or two from other departments and a couple he had met at university. He felt stupid though - he was soon turning 25 and felt like a love-sick puppy. The girls he had met were nice and while there was the occasional sleep over and 'friends with benefits' sex, he could not put Kes out of his mind.

Then the world changed. Perhaps, it was turned upside down.

It was a Friday lunchtime drink at the Old London that changed his life. He told his colleagues that he had to leave as some deadlines were imminent.

"Wait for me, I'll walk back with you," said Kes.

As they walked back to the office, a nervous Desmond asked for a date.

"I'm not good with dates; I have a boyfriend and besides, there are plenty of other girls in the office and I really don't know much about you," she said.

Desmond replied,

"True to say you don't know me but that can change. In terms of anyone else, I see you differently to the rest. Right now, you're the best friend I have here."

"That's all I need, a two-pot screamer," said Kes wryly.

"No, it's not like that, but I do know what I like – and that's you. I don't care about your boyfriend – just give me a chance."

Kes looked bewildered and then, with a sigh, just said,

"OK."

It wasn't the most exhilarating start, but Des was thrilled.

Chapter Seven

The first date between Kes and Desmond came with support in the form of Kes' girlfriend Cheryl acting as chaperone and the three had dinner at an Italian restaurant followed by a movie that the two ladies wanted to see. 'Annie Hall', the latest Woody Allen movie with Diane Keaton.

Desmond had worn a new suit, his second, for which he had squirreled away money and purchased from Fletcher Jones. He had always been told, if you are going to have a new suit, it should be from Fletcher Jones. He had dressed to impress even though the two ladies were wearing jeans. He thought how stupid he was to be dressed up in a three-piece suit on a casual Friday night.

After that, they all parted ways and while not ideal with Cheryl in tow, Desmond nevertheless headed off a very happy man. He wasn't going home that night, as he had planned to catch up with old friends on the Peninsula the next morning and had arranged to stay at a Mornington hotel. He had therefore driven into the CBD to head south the next day – but he was in glee mode. He savoured the brief kiss they had shared before departing, the brushing of their lips while Cheryl turned her back to provide some sense of privacy. Yes, he was on cloud nine. Make that nine point five.

That was the case until a taxi ran a red light, driving straight through his Ford Cortina. He found himself standing in St Kilda Road bleeding from his hand which had defensively pushed through the windscreen. His new suit was bloodied and torn at the knee.

Even in shock, he staggered across to the taxi that was in the middle of the intersection, to ensure there was life. The taxi driver seemed to be slumped over the steering wheel and the door was locked. Des tapped on the window and then realised, the driver was not slumped because he was unconscious, but in fact was on his radio to the taxi service administration.

His next memories consisted of an ambulance whose crew rushed past him to tend to the uninjured taxi driver, then the quick bandaging of his hand. Then all of a sudden he was in the front cabin of a tow truck carting his car to the tow company's yard.

Des shivered, not with the cold but through shock. The tow driver asked if he had a jacket and Des said,

"Yes, it's in the back of the car". The nameless driver retrieved his jacket and told Des to put it on, which the shaken Des did.

A call to his mate, Mick, saw Des safely picked up from a dirty, greasy wreckage depot in Windsor to a comfortable bed in Mt Eliza. After a few Scotches on the rocks with Mick, Des was able to sleep, for a short while at least.

Waking the next morning, Des a little groggy and uneasy on his feet, yet quickly taking stock of the night before. What a confused mess of emotions. Elation to nightmare in ten minutes. At that moment he felt like a tennis player who had won the first two sets in a grand slam and lost the next three.

There he was, just out of an unfamiliar bed, naked and a full length mirror on a cupboard door revealed more than he wanted to see. Bandaged hand, bruise to his right temple but more importantly, how did he get here?

A linen dressing gown draped at the end of the bed probably meant that Mick's more understanding wife, Margaret, had not only placed it there but potentially also put him to bed. Des sighed and then thought that one should swallow embarrassment as easily as humility.

He saw his crumpled suit tangled on a chair in the corner and examined the blood stains of his jacket and waist coat. He felt the jacket inside pockets and found them empty and suddenly came to the sickening realisation that his wallet was not there.

He walked out of the bedroom to be greeted by Mick and Margaret and their two-year old daughter, Shea.

"Well, look who has decided to join the living," said Mick cheerily.

"Yeah, righto," came Desmond's feeble reply.

"Want some breakfast or brunch - after all, it is eleven in the morning?" Margaret quizzed.

Des ignored that one and pretended to be totally normal, picking up the young Shea and giving her a kiss on the cheek before delicately placing her back on the play rug she was on.

"A coffee would be really good Margaret, if that's OK. But I need to use your phone as well," said Des.

"Coming right up. We aim to please, as we did last night," said Margaret with a wink that only made Des more anxious.

"You know where the phone is, don't you Des?" she added.

Des located the phone and rang a number that he had recalled to memory; had called it on and off, usually hanging up before it was answered.

"Hello," a female voice sounded down the line.

"Hello, can I speak to Kes?" asked Des.

"Kes? Oh you must be Desmond. It's Kes' mother, Alice," she replied.

"Hello, again, and nice to meet you," he stammered, nervousness kicking in big time.

"It's OK Desmond, my daughter tells me that she and Cheryl and you had a nice night."

Des's temperature and anxiety was still rising but the voice at the other end of the phone seemed to know this and had a semi-calming effect.

"I hope you will feel the same way when you meet me, Mrs. Swanson…"

"Call me Alice, I don't want to age that quickly."

"OK, Alice, can I please speak to your daughter, it's rather important?"

"Sure, I will just go and get her. I think she is studying in her bedroom," said Alice as she put the phone down.

A minute later or what seemed more like ten to Des, Kes' voice came on the line.

"Des? Why are you calling me at home? How did you get my number?" Kes fired the questions.

"Sorry Kes, I've had your number for weeks, always too scared to call but this is important."

"You know we are just getting to know each other, right?" said Kes.

"I know Kes, but I am a little dazed at the moment," replied Des.

"What do you mean?"

"You know after leaving you and Cheryl last night that I was heading down the Peninsula for the weekend?"

"Yes."

"I made it but not without a taxi ramming my car."

"Oh God, Des, are you alright?" Kes' voice rose with concern.

"Yes, thanks to friends that you must meet, they are godsends," said Des staring at his ever-curious, listening audience.

"As long as you are OK," said Kes.

"Mystery. Did I give you my wallet to put in your handbag at any stage last night..?"

"Why would you do that? I only had a clutch purse and you insisted on paying for everything, even though Cheryl and I tried to pay."

"And I wouldn't have it any other way, but that means I have been robbed by a tow-truck driver and I won't see the forty dollars I still had there and I'll have to cancel all cards and reorganise a new driver's licence."

"I'm so sorry Des, what can I do?"

"Stop being sorry for one thing, Kes, and accept my thanks for one of the best nights of my life," concluded Des.

"Yes, it was."

"Really?"

"I mean it was one of the best nights of my life too," said Kes. He could hear the smile in her voice.

Des hung up the phone and turned to the waiting audience of Mick and Margaret with the young Shea in her arms.

"Well?" asked the ever-pushy Margaret.

"Dead end on the wallet," said Des.

"Not what I'm after Des; more information?" pushed Margaret, laughing.

Des smiled. He could not help himself and then he started to chuckle.

Mick was amused. Mick was three years older than Des and he had not seen his friend in such a happy state for a long time. Mick in fact always showed some concern as he knew of Des' tough upbringing and what had often been hard times.

"What are you so fucking happy about; you've written off your car and been robbed in one hit," said Mick, breaking the brief silence by stating the obvious.

Des rubbed the forehead of toddler, Shea; walked up to Margaret and kissed her on both cheeks and then fronted his old mate with a kiss on the forehead.

"What the fuck are you doing, Dezzie?" Mick exclaimed.

"Mick, all is good. I just found the woman I am going to spend the rest of my life with."

Chapter Eight

The second date was even more interesting.

It mandated a visit to Kes' home to meet her parents.

Des had considered himself a cool customer until that critical moment he walked up to the door at 43 Lochart Street, Pascoe Vale South.

Kes met him at the door and he entered into unknown terrain. Sweat was starting to pour, anxiety was mounting, and his mouth was so dry; an unknown feeling for Des.

Kes' mother Alice was quick to come to the rescue, taking Desmond's hand in a light handshake and greeting him. Alice was not quite as tall as her daughter, but Desmond saw instantly where Kes got her good looks from.

Then Kes led Des by the hand into a dimly lit, small lounge room, where her father, Bruce, sat glued to a television screen

Des looked at the screen and saw Fitzroy playing against St Kilda in a Victorian Football League match. It was half time and Fitzroy were three points up.

Kes introduced Des with no motion from her father. Des held his hand out for the customary shake and a courteous greeting,

"Nice to meet you, Mr. Swanson," but Bruce remained still, transfixed on the television, not moving a muscle.

At one stage, Des thought that Bruce's pulse needed to be checked but the occasional rising of his chest suggested otherwise. In his mind, this was sheer rudeness; it didn't matter who he was, the acceptance of a hand-shake was a mandate in any polite society.

"It's very nice to meet you, sir," repeated the ever courteous Des.

Bruce did not budge so Des tried one more avenue.

"I think the 'Roy boys will get up, don't you?" posed Des.

Bruce turned his head and looked at Des as if he were totally insignificant.

"I was born and bred in St Kilda, so I don't think much of your predictions," said Bruce, finally breaking his silence.

"I'm sorry sir," said Des back-peddling, with Kes tugging at his arm to come out of the room.

Des, however, couldn't help himself with on final loudly spoken line.

"Bet you Fitzroy wins by more than five goals."

Bruce turned his head again, looked at Des and then affixed his gaze back on the television screen.

Des sighed but Kes had pushed him forward, whispering that her father was lying.

"He's always been a Roy Boy supporter, he's never lived in St Kilda and you should take it as a compliment that he even turned his head – that's what you were looking for, wasn't it?" asked Kes.

Des didn't respond but smiled at his date for the weekend. He did think of his past upbringing and worried that the father of the girl he had, in such a short time fallen in love with, could be a barrier in the future.

Bruce was not keen about Des and didn't understand how his daughter suddenly appeared to have two suitors.

With some small talk with her mother over and done with, Des escorted Kes to his new rental car, a very sporty Datsun 180B.

Des drove her to the Peninsula for the birthday celebration of an old high school friend. Des was upfront in saying that they would go to a Chinese restaurant and then drinks at his friend's house further down on the Peninsula. He asked if it was alright to book a motel in Mornington and was gracious to mention he would book two rooms.

Kes replied, "Two rooms would be an extravagant waste of money."

Desmond Jamieson was indeed in love.

Chapter Nine

The date was nothing more than remarkable. They had forgone the after-party celebrations, with a nudge and wink to Des from his friend Cecile who was hosting the party.

In his mind, lovemaking with Kes was just simply unbelievable. The passion which had started as soon as they entered the hotel room saw them collapse in each other's arms a few hours later and sleep finally overcame them; the rhythmic crashing of the waves outside resounded over and over.

The next morning, after another bout of lovemaking, Des drove Kes all around the Peninsula showing every sight to be seen; all of his past haunts, explaining what he got up to in his youth growing up on the Peninsula.

He took her to sites rarely seen by the hundreds of tourists that flocked to the area; one in particular, which had a spectacular view of both Port Phillip Bay and Westernport. This was a piece of vacant land coming off a track from the main road. Des said he didn't know who it belonged to but had always dreamed of buying it and building a home. Kes was in awe of the view and understood why Des was so taken by it.

Des then somewhat sadly and slowly drove Kes home, not wanting the weekend to end. Kes could sense this and merely said,

"Come on, show me what this car can really do." Des complied and put his foot down on the accelerator as soon as he got on the freeway.

***

Des went to work on the Monday, still in a state of semi-euphoria and when he saw Kes, he could see she was also in a very happy frame of mind.

By mid-morning, Kes had ventured up to Des with a file in hand as if to discuss a work matter. She slipped a folded note on to his desk and walked away. The note merely read – *The Moat for coffee after work?* He looked in her direction and gave a discreet nod.

The Moat was soon to become a late afternoon coffee or hot chocolate ritual. The café was divided into two sections; the front, where coffees and sandwiches were sold at lunchtime and a back section where a few small tables welcomed customers to dine in and sip their coffees.

The café closed at 6.30pm each evening but rarely were there any patrons after 5pm. Des never really understood the rationale for staying open later but he was truly appreciative that they did, particularly as the owners soon got used to the *Kes and Des show* and curtained the back section off. While they dutifully paid and sipped their beverage, the couple also used the time for kisses and warm embraces.

Then there was the issue of their work colleagues in the office; they both agreed that their new romance should leave them none the wiser. That soon proved to be naïve and rumours began but their colleagues reacted with no more than some light teasing. Even then, they still continued to act in clandestine fashion. Perhaps that was just part of the fun of the romance.

The weeks continued in some form of dreamy routine, including the odd stopping of the elevator mid-floor for an embrace, walking to the gardens up the road for lunch, and the odd night or two back at Des' apartment.

Then things changed.

Reality struck and did so with a big kick in the guts.

Kes took him aside and made it clear that while she had very much enjoyed their time together, due to her father's vocal insistence and potential engagement to another, even though there had been no proposal coming forth as yet, it was never going to work.

Des didn't need to be reminded of the latter. He was well aware his beloved was also still seeing someone else, but he just pretended not to care, which was in fact, furthest from the truth. He just didn't want to see Kes upset in any way.

He felt like he had been hit by lightning and didn't know how to respond. He walked away somewhat dumbfounded and unable to focus on his work, left the office early that afternoon.

He called into his local pub, a mere hundred yards or so from his flat. After his second pot of beer, his thoughts were certainly no clearer, and he made the conscious decision not to turn the situation into a sorrow-drowning exercise and went home.

After pacing his small flat over and over, he walked out and headed for the nearest phone booth. Putting forty cents into the slot, he quickly dialled Kes' number, only to be answered by the very gruff voice of Bruce.

"Is Kes there please?" he asked, almost pleading.

"No she's not and *her name is not Kes,*" was the reply and then heard the phone go dead.

He forlornly returned to his flat and wondered if a few more pints would be in order. Then there was an unexpected knock and when he opened the door, there was Kes, tears filling her eyes.

"I'm sorry," she blurted, "I don't want to lose you but there is just so much pressure."

He didn't say anything, just took her in his arms and held her ever so close.

The secret dates continued albeit on a less frequent basis.

Kes was very reverent towards her father and there was also a guilt that she struggled with as she had been going out with her 'real' boyfriend for some years. Both of their work commitments and studies also made it hard.

Des, regardless of a constant fear of losing her, resumed playing the waiting game with a belief that things would work out. After all, he loved her, and he believed she loved him.

Of course, there was William, aka Bill, the boyfriend himself. Bill was born with the silver spoon in his mouth and was promising the world to Kes.

There was no doubt that Bruce thought that Bill represented future wealth that would rightfully cater for his daughter, while he saw Des as a nobody who had not yet made his mark and would struggle to do so.

Des considered Bill to be unworthy and made it fairly clear to Kes of his thoughts and intentions to be her partner.

In the meantime, Bill was slowly becoming aware that feelings were being held between Des and his potential betrothed. Bill had no intention of giving way.

Des had tried to convince Kes of the need to confirm where her heart rested. Des was a true romantic and he would spend time each night writing prose that he would give Kes the next day. Reading his love letters, warm joy curled up inside Kes' heart. She hid them all in a secret shoe-box under her bed.

However, it was getting harder and often, following their hot chocolate visit to The Moat, he would walk Kes back towards the office, only to relinquish his beloved to the hands of Bill in his despised Mercedes.

Des decided to 'befriend' Bill one day, post-Moat, and attempt to engage in conversation. Some stupid idiom about keeping your enemies closer kept sticking in his mind.

Unfortunately, Bill was not appeased by the constant tapping on his car's roof from the nervous Des' opal ring, as he talked through the window. Bill wasn't even listening to the forced idle chatter that Des was adopting, and Des was not even conscious he was tapping – it was more of a nervous reaction as he tried to make dialogue. Evidently a Mercedes deserved better treatment and Bill, getting out of the vehicle, threw the first punch – Des, taken by utmost surprise, fell to the ground.

In true boxing style, Des got up to resist and signalled he was up for a rematch.

Bill was happy for the invitation and threw a second punch, missing the defendant's jaw. Des took control, landing a swift fist to Bill's midriff and a second to his right jaw. Game over.

That was when the sadness hit as to his surprise, Kes helped the crumpled Bill get up and back into the car. Kes just looked stunned at first and then just glared at Des in a *'how dare you'*, kind of way. The dazed Bill had enough sense remaining to drive off with haste

There was silence at the work front for some days that followed. Des tried to apologise by saying he had learned to defend himself at the boxing gym at a young age and was sorry for the outcome. He kept saying to himself, *I should have laid down on the road and stayed there.* That's what he wanted to say to Kes, but he couldn't get to first base to convey the message

The silence was deafening, and he could see Kes just living in her own world; she started to look tired. So Des worked even harder to fulfil some of Kes' duties after hours so she could focus on her studies; he could at least give her space and protection.

The result was the tantalising promise for a promotion, which was a mere whisper amongst the staff, as if there was some kind of bizarre competition via a secret ballot, which ultimately went to Kes. Her manager threw his arms up in the air with jubilation, announcing her promotion to the whole department.

The blushing Kes stared straight at Des. She was blushing but was definitely not happy. Perhaps the blush concealed steam within. She signalled with two fingers pointing down in a walking motion. This was the signal that she wanted to talk in the stairwell at least two floors down. Des returned the signal with a simple yet, slow lowering of his eyes.

Des thought that finally Kes was going to show her temper over the thrashing he had given Bill and then there would be silence between them forever more.

When they met mid-way between floors, Kes was clearly upset.

"I'm so sorry, Des," said Kes.

Des was taken aback and then it clicked. He knew exactly what she was referring to. It was the promotion.

"It's OK, you deserve it," said Des.

"No. I should tell the truth. It's been your extra work because you were looking after me."

Thinking about it, Des wasn't exactly happy about the promotion, but he also considered his own manager to be a weak, egotistical individual who couldn't recognise the talent he actually had in his own division which certainly included him. Besides, his love for Kes was too great and had not been tarnished by silence or the accolades he, himself, may have deserved.

"Stop worrying about it; just enjoy the moment," he said softly as he put his arms around her.

"I'm sorry for the silent treatment," said Kes looking down at her shoes as if they needed a polish.

"It's OK. I know you're angry with me. I'm sorry. I had to learn to defend myself at a young age."

"Well, you certainly did that."

"I shouldn't have gotten up, turned the other cheek and all that."

"No, I don't believe that. I hate violence and I have to admit, Bill deserved what he got, but in his mind he was defending his honour."

"Honour can be such a burden. Think of all that have fallen over the centuries for the sake of honour and let's face it, quite often honour is just another fancy word for self-indulgent pride."

Kes took his words in, thought of their wisdom, almost philosophical.

"Please, I don't want to talk about Bill," she said, somewhat feebly.

Des could tell not to push the envelope any further than he just had. At least she was speaking to him again. After a hesitant pause, like dead air-time on radio, he broke the silence.

"So, the Moat after work..?"

"Sure," said Kes, finally smiling, accompanied by a deep sigh.

Chapter Ten

The next morning, there was no conversation about the evening prior when Des had dutifully walked Kes back toward the office, to the waiting Mercedes.

Des had deliberately smiled and given the thumbs up to Bill, whose head remained looking straight ahead. This was Des playing dirty in a worthless psychological game and he felt a little ashamed of himself, but he also believed he was in a battle for the one prize he wanted more than life itself; to win Kes over, forever.

Instead, of covering old ground from the day before, Kes merely asked Desmond to accompany her to the university at lunchtime.

"There should be exam results posted on the noticeboard and I don't think I want to be alone. Just a quick tram ride and we will be back within the hour," pleaded Kes. Des needed no more persuasion.

They sped up the street to catch a tram and on arrival at the stop outside the university, Kes grabbed Des' hand to get to the corridor where the results were waiting. Her grip on his hand was so strong, he wondered if he would get the circulation back in his fingers.

There was a queue leading up to a noticeboard in the undercover campus area and Des kept their place in the line whilst Kes paced up and down like a caged tiger focussed on one thing and one thing only - escape from the confinement of uncertainty.

Finally, there they were, searching up and down through a myriad of names and results. Distinction. High Distinction. Distinction. High-fives all round.

Kes was ecstatic and let Des know with a long, passionate kiss.

On the way back to the office, the tram ride seemed to take that much longer. Kes was still beaming but Des couldn't help but notice how tired she looked. At first, he thought it was the adrenalin rush after awaiting the results for all of her toil and studying, but he couldn't but think that there was much more than that. The strain of her work, studies and two lovers was showing. That was his conclusion.

Yet, Kes had practically dragged him up onto a tram ride to feel her nervousness, and to share the celebration of her excellence, her finest academic tribute so far. She hadn't asked Bill but he, Desmond Jamieson, to accompany her. Surely that was important?

He felt every part of her feelings, her tremors and fears, her goals and triumphs, her vulnerability; yes, most of all, her vulnerability.

What suddenly dawned on him most was that she was born in a different world to the one he was born in.

She had many caring for and loving her. Her wonderful, warm-hearted mother, Alice, who had a soft spot for Des, her obstinate father, Bruce, who despite his gruffness, cherished and wanted to protect his daughter - even the stuck-up Bill, who if Des was in his shoes, would do anything to fight for this woman.

God help me, I'm even feeling empathy for that prick.

He had learnt to protect himself but other than his younger sister Lee, he had never protected another human being. Lee ended up a tragic loss he would never forget, but her demise was not from lack of his protection. He believed he was capable of doing just that, of protecting and loving.

This time, he would be more capable of doing so.

"I need you to book yourself with me tomorrow night; is that OK?" asked Des, making up his mind.

This was a very considered approach and Des himself could not believe the gamble he was taking.

"That could work, I guess. I owe you for today - not just the promotion thing but you being with me here, right now, on this tram. There is no one else I would have wanted to take with me to get my results. What are you thinking?" asked Kes.

"I'll let you know tomorrow morning. I just have to make some arrangements, but bring a change of clothes."

"OK, and thank you for being you."

"I love you, Kes."

He gave a most fervent kiss before getting off the tram and they walked back to the office.

Des was silent after that, deep in thought, but he could see his Kes starting to fade under the pressure and it was time to change things before it got the better of her.

***

Chapter Eleven

Lauren Black's office in City General Hospital was conservative to say the least.

Actually, calling it conservative would be considered generous. It was tiny.

Lauren was five foot eight in height but was graced with a slender body which comfortably slipped past the single four-drawer filing cabinet as she sat down behind her desk. There, neatly arranged, were a telephone, lap-top computer, in-tray and a tin cup containing several pens, a permanent marker, a pair of scissors and a staple remover. Next to the tin cup was a glass jar filled with hundreds of small pieces of different coloured paper.

She hit the start button on her lap-top and surveyed her small office.

There were two visitor chairs on the opposite side of the desk. These were for family members, and used in the many debriefs during the final hours of one or another of her patients.

The desk also had two lockable drawers; the first with a tray full of paper clips, bulldog clips, a stapler, a notepad and a small stack of index cards. The second drawer held some paracetamol tablets, a small box of tampons and a bottle of brandy.

The brandy was for self-medicinal purposes of course, only if required and in the most extreme circumstances, and of course, completely against all company regulations.

She sat behind her desk while the computer was springing to life. As she did, she glanced at the small noticeboard on the wall to her left. This had become part of her daily ritual.

Pinned to the right top corner of the board was a laminated page of the hospital's values and behaviours. Adjacent to that was the fire escape plan showing the path one was to take if such an event were to take place and in the centre of the board was an index card with hand-written scrawl in black.

The card simply read:

"Courage is what it takes to stand up and speak; courage is also what it takes to sit down and listen." ~ Winston Churchill.

Toward the lower left corner of the board several photos were pinned, overlapping each other. This was her personal collage.

Lauren cast her eyes over the small collection of photographs, some a little frayed, one torn in half. The daily ritual continued. It gave her some level of solace, particularly during the most stressful of days.

Amongst the photos, she knew there was one constant. Her ever-smiling daughter, Eileen.

Eileen had been given the middle name of the child's grandmother. The photos, if put together, showed a timeline that most would not capture quickly.

There was a photo of Eileen and Lauren at a Port Douglas beach with palm trees and blue sky background – that was only three years ago. Another photo covered the generations, including the two of them along with Lauren's mother. That photo was taken two years ago on the last day of Eileen's primary school years.

There were other photos of Eileen at varying ages including the most recent high school photo. And there was the torn photo of her as a baby; the other half of the print had held the image of Eileen's father, Lauren's cheating, abusive bastard of an ex-husband.

Eileen was now the proverbial twelve-going-on-thirty years

of age; knowing all and knowing nothing. In twelve months' time she would shed her steely grin and the dental braces would be removed. Her long braided brown hair would give way to new fashion that only a precocious teenager could and would demand. Lauren knew it well. She, perhaps, had not been that different at Eileen's age.

Lauren's trip down memory lane, looking at her personal photo collage was short lived as the hospital's insignia and log on entry screen appeared on the computer screen.

She quickly tapped in her user-name of LBlack and her password of Eileen07. She knew that in a month's time it would end in 08, then 09 and after that, she would have to rethink her memorable password pattern.

She never really understood the security level requirement but considered there were enough people in the world with mischief on their minds to do damage.

The home intranet page came up, promoting the wonderful organisation it was, the motto of *'providing care for people and life'* now a little staid in her mind, but she held on to it every day just the same. She believed in doing the best for the patients.

Her patients, however, were different from the norm. They were not having gall stones or appendixes removed. They had gone beyond the heart attack or stroke phase.

Her patients. Her clients. They were real people with no hope left. Their kidney, liver or heart could not be replaced. They were real people who were going to die. The *'and life'* part of the motto was a little redundant but she did hold on to it just the same, after all when one client dies, there are the loving survivors left behind.

She clicked on to the Outlook email icon and waited for the screen to come up.

There were several new messages, including five from administration advising of network upgrades and a planned fire drill. Why they announced a planned fire evacuation made no sense to her. Half the people who knew of the planned fire drill would leave the building and head for the café two doors down; the other half were lemmings and just followed the directions of the man or woman with the red helmet.

As far as Lauren was concerned, they should start a real fire and see if the drills had any effect. Having thought that, she knew that would end in tragedy, so she moved her thoughts beyond the stupid email, pushing delete instead.

As she trawled through the list of emails, she noted one from her mother. The email addressee was labelled Caitlin Black. Having had some doubts about bringing her mother into the new tech generation, providing her with internet and email and all the havoc it could bring, she opened the email.

Hi Lorrie, isn't this fun, I can now email you. I hope I have got it right. Can you please reply so I know you have received this message?

Love, Mum.

Lorrie was the name given to Lauren at a young age; firstly by friends and then adopted by her mother. Lauren smiled at that. She hit the reply button and typed, *Loud and clear. See you tomorrow night. Love, L.*

Just as she did so, the incoming beep sounded. A new email from none other than Amelia Schwartz herself. Not just an email, but a meeting request.

Why would the CEO want to meet with me? She hit the enter key and opened the email.

> Lauren,
>
> *I understand you are very busy with an active case load, but I would appreciate if we could meet at 4.30 this afternoon. I wish to discuss your most recent patient, Mr Desmond Jamieson.*
>
> *Regards*
>
> *Amelia Schwartz*
>
> *Chief Executive Officer*
>
> *MGH*

Lauren read the meeting request over and over. Amelia Schwartz - AS. God, I'm stupid.

She swiftly hit the reply button, accepting the invitation.
I don't even know the guy yet. Who the hell is Mr Desmond
Jamieson?

***

Chapter Twelve

Jack Bissen, with his balding scalp and shaggy hair on three sides, waited at the corner of Rose and Smith Streets, as he had done many times before.

This was his day. A score to be made. A few hundred dollars to feed his addiction. Of course, his business was self-perpetuating; make a score to have a score.

And there it was. A car turning into Rose Street. Obviously two teenagers and the boy was driving daddy's BMW.

These rich kids, he thought. *Looking for the sales.* In his mind they were to be taught a lesson. A lesson that it's not all easy.

He walked around the corner, watched the Beamer park twenty metres along the street, and slowly moved to the passenger side of the car.

They did not see him but as the young girl was getting out of the car, he grabbed her with his arm around her waist and a switch blade pointing to her throat. She gave a shriek, but it was quickly muffled by his large hand over her mouth as he pushed her against the car.

The teenage boy on the other hand was absolutely stunned. He had gotten out of the car at the same time as his girlfriend and was totally startled with what lay before him.

"What the fuck, man?" his voice much shriller that he would ever recognise. Fear does that to your voice.

In the meantime, his girlfriend was squirming in muscular vice-type grip.

"Let me make it easy, then I won't kill her, and I *may* not kill you," said Bissen, almost listlessly, uncaring and practiced. He had this down pat.

"Anything, man, anything – just let her go."

Bissen softly spoke into the girl's ear,

"Scream and I will kill you."

He took his hand away from her mouth, tears starting to stream down her face as she sobbed in fear. He slowly let his hand trace down the girl, feeling her left breast.

"Nice titties."

His hand continued down the girl's body, raising her short skirt.

"Please, let her go."

Bissen looked at the pleading boy, tears starting to form in his very young eyes.

"Sure kid, throw me your wallet."

The teenager did exactly that and Bissen caught it with his left hand, his body hard against the girl pinned to the side of the car.

"And what's in the console, kid, give me that too."

"Just CDs."

"Yep, I'll take them and the extra cash too."

The boy didn't even wonder how this thug knew that the console had more cash. He just handed it over, his hands sweaty and shaking as he did so.

Two minutes later, Bissen walked away with three CDs and six hundred in cash. He left them with a threat, as he glanced at the driver's licence in the wallet; a threat he knew to be idle, but the terrified, unsuspecting youth did not; *"Don't go to the cops, coz I know where you live."*

Two hundred he put into the left inside pocket of his denim jacket. That would more than cover the right honourable senior constable Fagan of the Fitzroy police.

He almost chortled to himself as he often did; an unreal sort of reaction to the aftermath of the adrenaline spent and the fresh hit of drugs awaiting him.

In his mirth he thought of his ex-wife and the child that he had no genuine feeling for. She now despised him and sometimes he regretted his actions, but he knew that this was his life. It served him well enough. *Perhaps I should call by and see how she's going and that brat of a kid too.*

***

Chapter Thirteen

Caitlin Black also smiled when she read her daughter's reply.

She smiled for two reasons. Firstly for getting a response from her daughter in the first place, knowing how busy she was. Secondly, for letting her daughter assume she was nigh-on computer illiterate. She promised herself to let her daughter know the truth one day soon.

The technology connection had been a form of additional bonding between the two women. There was no doubt that the technology had changed over the years, but it wasn't so hard to grasp for her active mind.

Caitlin at sixty-six years of age was a most independent woman. Her tall, slender figure had indeed endured the test of time.

Every two months, she still had her hair treated in a golden, honey-blonde shade. She had no wish to see the inevitable grey of women of her age. Her original mousey-brown hair was long gone, and she believed in keeping up appearances.

She clicked off the email screen and opened the web browser to access her Facebook page. Here she would at least catch up the latest gossip of her granddaughter, Eileen.

Eileen was full of life and smart. She was a good girl in her grandmother's eyes. Some new photos of Eileen and her friends came to life on the screen before her.

Some chat notes starting with OMG which Caitlin had worked out to be Oh My God, with details of a boy she had befriended at school. *Absolutely gorgeous, I think I am in love.*

OMG was exactly what Caitlin thought. She logged out of Facebook and put the computer into sleep mode.

She looked around her study abound with photos on the walls. Photos of Lauren and Eileen at various stages.

One photo of Lauren at her graduation always brought a smile and sometimes a tear. She had been so proud of Lauren getting her psychology degree and with High Distinction levels at that. Yet, she was sometimes troubled that her daughter was dealing with the dying rather than helping the living. It didn't seem right.

Caitlin looked at her bookcase, not more than a metre wide but towering to the ceiling, making her study all that smaller in reality. All of her favourite books sat there. The red covered book in particular was her favourite and she never tired of re-reading it. Looking at the tower of books, she thought, it's time I dusted.

Chapter Fourteen

Lauren had done her rounds, catching up with her case load. She had four cases including the new arrival, Des Jamieson.

She was pleased to note that the other three were in reasonable spirit with the small exception of Phil Barclay who had no idea where he was or in fact, who he was. For Phil, it was a matter of days if not hours, but Lauren was realistic in knowing that she may not be able to achieve much for Mr Barclay.

The other two, Gwen Davidson and Marshal McLean were indeed in reasonable spirits considering their impending fate.

Gwen had liver cancer beyond all realms of surgery or recovery. In her first meeting with Gwen, Lauren learned that she had partied hard and had indeed had much to celebrate over her 71 years.

She had six grandchildren from three daughters and to her glee, two of her grandchildren were boys. She proudly told the story of her grandchildren and how the female lineage had finally been broken.

"Not that there is anything wrong with the girls in the family, but I wish my Donald had lived to see these kids. I am sure he would have been taking those boys camping and fishing if he were still alive," she had confided to Lauren.

Lauren thought that Gwen would be a wait and see in terms of her good humour. It was often a telling sign that things would unravel, and rightfully so. Grief would hit at some stage. In the meantime, Lauren had cleared the way to ensure her children and grandchildren had as much access rights as possible.

That was the beauty of the ResiCare. People facing their final days could be visited night and day by their loved ones, regardless of the time. However, Lauren was a stickler for knowing the comings and goings of said loved ones and insisted on a signing-in process for the visitor's book.

After all, there had been the odd occasion that the loved one had taken it upon him or herself to bring a shortening of the patient's life and euthanasia, whilst Lauren thought to be fair and reasonable in some cases, was still illegal and as such, against ResiCare policy. It was also a fact that some so-called loved ones were only maintaining an active interest because of potential inheritance of the family wealth.

Such was the case with Annette Sinclair, a wealthy spinster with greedy nephews and nieces. They had come to visit their aunt frequently once they had learned of her impending demise. Of course, they were furious to learn the day after her death, that she, of sound mind and body, had left close to two million dollars to the Sacred Heart Mission.

Marshal McLean was a totally different specimen and would no doubt offer Lauren a different sort of challenge. Marshal was only 28 years of age and a plumber by trade.

He was extremely handsome and physically very fit. When Lauren first met Marshal, she thought there had been a mistake, but the cerebral aneurysm had taken its toll and with a closer look, one could tell of the impact of the stroke affecting his left side and making his mouth slightly twisted.

The problem for Marshal was the blood haemorrhage to his brain which caused the stroke, and had also leaked further into the lower cranium. They had tried to release the pressure but to no avail. Young Marshal McLean was dying at a fast rate.

It was in such cases, that Lauren thought of euthanasia but to her surprise, Marshal still had some wits about him. His speech was impaired but managed to drawl and also write.

He said he knew he was going to die but he believed in reincarnation and that he would be back. He started to scrawl a letter to his parents who were stricken with grief and another to his girlfriend who he had planned to propose to just before the stroke. Lauren had helped him by being there to listen to his words of love and told him she would type up the letters and make sure that his loved ones would receive them.

Then there was Desmond Jamieson, whom she was yet to learn about. When she called by to see her new patient, however, he was fast asleep. Not surprising as he had insisted coming off the tubes with one drip remaining that provided as much painkilling medication as possible.

She glanced at her watch; 4.20 and she started to quicken her steps, knowing she had to be in the administration building in time to meet Amelia Schwartz.

Take care of this patient; a major supporter of this facility. The words kept filling her head. She had not had enough time to study her new patient.

I know sweet FA about him. Probably not the answer I should go in with.

Still the words scribed by AS stuck in her mind as she picked up her pace and headed to the South Wing where the administration, finance and brain trust of the organisation hid, well away from the day to day operations of the hospital.

Well away from the sick and the dying.

***

Lauren was sitting in the reception area just outside the office of the chief executive. She had made it with two minutes to spare but had now been sitting nervously for the past six minutes.

Then the door opened and a dumpy, five foot two woman presented herself. This was the power woman, Amelia Schwartz, with tortoiseshell-rimmed glasses with thick lenses swinging on a beaded chain around her neck.

Lauren had met her on only three previous occasions, twice at hospital fund-raising events, the other in front of a mediation exit interview with the family of Jim Trevallis. The latter had given Lauren a true appreciation of this stout, formidable woman's skills.

Lauren had explained that she had done everything possible for Jim Trevallis. The family, still grieving, were asking whether his final days could have been more comfortable. *Comfortable and dignified.*

Enter Amelia Schwartz into the conversation. She had firmly put forward a most compelling argument, one of Jim Trevallis' mindset, his turmoil with the very family who were trying to gain some level of compensation for their grief. The family, led by Jim's sister, Katrina, left without another word.

"Come in please, Lauren," Amelia greeted, offering her hand to shake, which Lauren readily accepted.

Inside the CEO's office, they sat in armchairs facing each other across a coffee table. On the table was the latest edition of BRW, a copy of the in-house employee magazine, *In Care,* and a landscaping magazine entitled *Garden World* which seemed out of place to Lauren.

"You're looking well, Lauren," Schwartz observed with a pleasant smile, "I take it that you are still enjoying the role."

"Indeed, I am," said Lauren, then nervously adding, "You're looking well yourself."

The last statement was a lie. In fact, Lauren perceived Amelia as being over-tired, overstressed and most unhappy.

"Well it's interesting times," said Amelia, gazing across the office toward her desk as if she had forgotten something.

She had in fact, just finished with a most disagreeable conversation with the chairman of the board and was still pondering her position. The argument was about how the palliative care unit, PalCare, would operate if further financial restraints were introduced.

The professional Amelia Schwartz then kicked in, placing her tortoiseshell-rimmed glasses squarely on the bridge of her nose, her keen blue eyes now clearly focussed on the person across the table.

"I'm sorry to have kept you waiting Lauren, but I thought it important that we meet to discuss your new patient, Des Jamieson," she started.

"Sure."

"What do you know about Mr Jamieson?"

The words resounded: *Take care of this patient; a major supporter of this facility.* Her earlier thought of *sweet FA* also came to mind.

"To be fair, Ms Schwartz..."

"Please call me Amelia, I detest formality."

"To be fair, Amelia, I have not had a chance to have a real conversation. He insisted on the catheters be removed and I am not sure he will have the strength that he thinks he will."

"He is a remarkable human being, so don't be too surprised."

"You obviously know him, Amelia. Can you fill me in?"

Take care of this patient; a major supporter of this facility.

"Did you write on his chart?" asked Lauren.

"Yes, I know Des Jamieson and yes, I wrote the special comment on his med-chart. In fact, I have my job here thanks to him. So do you."

"What do you mean?"

"Des Jamieson was the chairman of the board a decade ago. He gave me the job but much more than that.

"He insisted on creating a well-being centre for the children, and a proactive palliative care centre for the dying – what we knew then as the Patient Palliative Care Unit, and in more recent years, rebranded as PalCare. Hence, you have a job because he created it."

"I see."

"No you don't, not yet. Jamieson drove it as a mission that people should have the opportunity to depart from this earth with dignity," said Amelia.

"Comfort and dignity," said Lauren.

"Exactly. But he created a world first here at City General. He then went on to fight government to include the facility in the medical tax-free threshold and guess what? He succeeded, making it feasible to provide quality services to the dying, regardless of their status in life."

Whilst very direct in her address, Amelia Schwartz could not help but feel the emotion behind her words. She rubbed her right eye beneath the thick lens and then continued with her semi-prepared thoughts.

"You do a damn good job here Lauren, but I am not sure you are up to a Des Jamieson assignment."

"What do you mean?"

"I think he will be pig-headed, not like the Trevallis case. That was just plain stupid, but I think he will try and manipulate everything around him."

"Many try, Amelia, but let me say, I am no slouch in my management of my patients," said Lauren almost defiantly.

"I appreciate your words, your professionalism and your effort, but the Board is looking for changes and without Des Jamieson's influence, they could close the ResiCare or charge extreme costs to families."

"They can't do that. You said yourself that Mr Jamieson fought for the tax-free agenda."

"They can and they will. Boards can be very greedy."

"So, I don't understand. Are you telling me I may not have a job?"

"Not at all, dear. I am defying all around me and giving you specific instructions to give Des Jamieson the best service you can. I owe him that and so do you. And to hell with the rest."

Chapter Fifteen

Lauren finished her meeting with CEO, Amelia Schwartz, with that final question from her boss, "So what's your strategy?" still ringing through her mind.

Her answer was simplistic. *"Truth."* When asked what that meant, she merely repeated, *"Truth."*

"I know you want me to look after him, obviously more than anyone else, but if he was the creator *of what we do, do you think he would want to be treated any differently?"*

She had made her point.

"My strategy is simple, let them go with dignity and to do so, let them go with no regrets."

The meeting concluded not with a simple handshake but with the short, stubby woman giving a hug and a kiss to her cheek. Lauren had made her point and by God she knew she had to make it happen in reality.

She decided to pass by Des Jamieson's room one more time. He was still asleep, so she called by the nurses' quarters which doubled as the ward's reception, leaving instructions to call her if required.

This was her normal way of advising that she was heading home for the day, after which she would drop by her office to shut down her laptop and then leave the hospital. However, she did stress that she wanted to be contacted regarding anything out of the norm with her new patient, particularly as it was Saturday tomorrow and she was not on the roster.

Chapter Sixteen

The following morning, Des informed Kes ("Des and Kes" – it had a nice ring to it, thought Des, even if it did sound a little corny) that they were booked into the Hilton on the Park.

Kes was thrilled by the prospect, but Des was feeling trepidation to say the least. This would be his one last-ditch effort to secure the love of his dreams and his life.

A candle-lit dinner at the traditional French restaurant, unimaginatively called Frenchies, set the scene for some pleasant and also awkward conversation.

"I think you know that I love you, Kes," said Des.

"Yes, I do," replied a blushing, almost twitching, Kes.

"And you? How do you feel about me?"

"I love you too, Des."

"So… can you imagine our lives together?"

"Yes, I can, but you need to know, my family, my father especially; they are driving me insane. Bill has done nothing wrong, except for trying to take you out with a punch that time, and by the way, that hasn't helped my father's thinking – he now thinks you're just a thug."

"I said I was sorry. I usually don't hit back but this was different; I love you and I think you are just a charm bracelet for that prick. I normally don't hit shit like him because shit splatters."

Kes couldn't help a titter of laughter.

"Sorry," said Des.

Then Kes got a little more serious.

"I also want a professional life, I have worked so hard for it and over time I also want children," she said.

"I never thought otherwise but we have to decide on their names."

"Their names?"

"Well I like Shaun and something almost traditional like Laurence for boys; Shea, like my goddaughter or again, classical such as Catherine for girls; what about you?"

"They all sound fine to me."

"I think we should skip dessert, don't you?" posed Des.

What followed was a night of lovemaking that Des could only ever dream of. But while Des was mellowing towards a comfortable sleep, Kes sat up, with fears about her future coursing through her mind.

The next morning, again with love arousing between them, there was much happiness until Des broke their warm cocoon of silence.

"So what about it?" asked Des.

"About what?" replied Kes.

"I want to marry you, Kes. I love you and know we will have a great future together." There, he'd said it.

Kes hesitated, brows creased and drew back. Des knew in that instant that the final blow was coming.

"I love you, Des, but it would kill my father and I have Bill to consider," said Kes.

"So that's it?" asked Des.

"What do you mean?"

"Kes, I have watched you turn from a vibrant, beautiful person into an exhausted, hollow woman. You think you're stuck between me and Bill but only you can make that choice. I can't hang around, watching the person I love deteriorate before my eyes. I love you, more than anybody, but the only way I can break this deadlock is to leave you," said Des, his words catching in his throat.

"You can't mean this," said Kes, tears starting to stream down her cheeks.

"You will remember that I love you, Kes. You will remember me from time to time as your life unfolds. I am leaving for Queensland in the morning; my transfer is confirmed."

Des gave her one final kiss, moist with her tears and walked out of the hotel room. It wasn't until he stepped out to the footpath outside that his own tears started to flow and steadily so.

Chapter Seventeen

Des Jamieson's mind was suddenly filled with dismay; a grief that took him beyond his own impending fate but then he thought, that was the point of it after all - to think about others and not dwell on his own demise. He assumed that to be the name of the game.

Here he was, lying in a hospital bed, devoid of all he loved.

And what of his beloved Kes whom he had never heard from again? She had undoubtedly married the Mercedes boy, Bill, but was she in fact still alive, or gone on ahead as he was destined to do?

A single tear fell from his right eye. But he wasn't yet prepared to weep, not fully anyway.

Had he got everything right? Did he have everything in order and was he the master of order he was renowned to be? He had built a profession based on two elements; knowledge of your stakeholders' needs and order. He had built an empire on these two elements and yes, he admitted to himself, with a little luck on the way.

He had climbed the corporate charts quickly. Had gained his accounting degrees, a Master of Business Administration and several diplomas and was known for his intelligence, yet here he was pondering death which was an unanswerable phenomenon. Education and achievements meant very little at this point of time.

So far he had cancelled out one wife and any surviving next of kin but that wasn't true, was it?

There was a son and a daughter to think about.

He hadn't spoken to Ryan for five, or was it six months and Fiona, who detested him, for three years. When he had last spoken to Ryan he did not share the truth about his illness those past months, nor did he give any indication of his fears about the months to come.

Ryan was always up for a chat, but Desmond also recognised that it was he that always had to make the phone call. Ryan was his first born, and in fact his only born from his third marriage; a marriage that he had considered as happy as a marriage could be. His second marriage was a very regrettable and costly mistake.

His first wife, Janice Lee, was an angel and she had died giving birth to a still-born daughter. He had so much hope for his prospective daughter, but it was not to be, and at that time he had lost the most beautiful wife and the only genuine love he had felt since Kes.

The one thing Jamieson could never come to grips with was not having someone by his side and ultimately, he chased after partners and had a few affairs along the way. His love for Janice Lee, however, was unsurpassed, except for his first true love for Kes.

His second wife, Vivian, was a disaster from the start, and the mother of his step-daughter, Fiona. It was true to say that Vivian was the genuine proverbial gold-digger and had lured him unwittingly to a very expensive divorce. He had tried desperately to be a positive influence on Fiona, whom he had treated as his biological daughter, buying her a very expensive education and everything else she ever wanted for that matter.

Fiona, however, was the apple of her mother's eye, not his. She snubbed her step-father as soon as the divorce proceedings settled, happily clinging to her mother instead.

After Vivian, there had been numerous other women in

Desmond's life along the way until he met his third and final wife, Carol. Carol was a good fit and he regretted not paying more attention to her. Carol gave him a son, and he thought the world of Ryan but again, not enough attention, always away with work commitments and then he realised his son had grown up and flown the coop before he woke up. Regrets and more regrets.

Ryan was a special investigations officer with the Federal Police, based in Darwin. He mainly focused on narcotics coming into the country and kept a careful watch on traffic from South East Asia.

Des was proud of his son but never really discussed his son's work. Two years ago, it came a little too close, however, when Ryan had good reason to call his father regarding an acquaintance, William Chen.

Ryan had recalled his father speaking of Chen in terms of property dealings and Desmond openly admitted to his son that he knew William Chen, but in his opinion the Singaporean magnate had no drug dealings within his empire.

Des, knowing William well, believed what he was telling his son was the truth. There were never any drugs in Chen's dealings; only massive property transactions and many of them.

Ryan had asked about the basis of their acquaintance and Des had been honest in saying he had audited accounts and carried out genuine business transactions with Chen over the past two decades.

Des was concerned about the crossover between his business dealings and his personal life at the time. He had been trying hard to build as many bridges as possible with his son and others for that matter, but the introduction of Will Chen's name into that space was unexpected and not welcomed.

Des called Chen to suss out concerns without mentioning his son, and in his last conversation with his son on the matter, the whole issue had dissolved. It was an aspirin in water; there had been a headache and then nothing the next day. Des had only hoped that his long-term acquaintance had not lied to him. Ryan never mentioned the Chen name again to his father.

It was while Desmond Jamieson contemplated his son, Ryan, that the next wave of exhaustion hit him and as he drifted off to sleep, Ryan was in the forefront, Will Chen loomed nearby and a very bloody hotel room came from the depths of his mind.

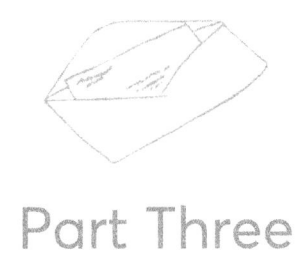

Part Three

The beginning of an empire

"There will come a time of fire and night, when enemies rise and empires fall, when the stars themselves begin to die."

Kevin J. Anderson

Chapter Eighteen

Desmond's tenure in the Brisbane bureau had been short-lived. He was already regretting the stance he had taken with Kes. He had prayed and he had gambled on her following him, but he quickly realised that his prayers were to be unanswered and also that he was a terrible gambler. However, he was also true to his word and did not try to contact her. He had genuine concerns over her wellbeing, and he couldn't bear to be part of her decline any further.

Almost as soon as he got to Queensland, an opportunity came up that would see him in South East Asia for several years, particularly in Thailand, Vietnam and most regularly, in Singapore.

It was in Singapore he met William Chen. William, born Huang Xiaou, was a Chinese entrepreneur who dealt in property sales and exporting of goods. Will, as he preferred to be called, had been referred to Des through another business contact, Glen Smithers.

Will was looking for an auditor for his portfolio of several companies. Des fitted the bill, but Will was a cautious businessman when it came to investing his trust, so he called for a meeting which was basically an interview. Des wasn't particularly fussed with the approach but had promised Glen he would go to the meeting.

While Des was nonchalant about the meeting, not caring whether he gained the client or not, he was quickly converted.

In ten minutes, Will had fired off enough questions to convince Des of how shrewd a businessman William Chen was.

Chen had asked the normal and expected questions of Des; his background, who had he provided services to in the past, knowing that Des was only 28 years of age. Then he turned things up a notch, asking what Des wanted out of life.

Des was taken aback as, for the first time in his life, he was not sure of the answer. Chen was only four years older than Des, but he read the younger person's face and saw the puzzled look.

"I will ask the question again," said Chen. "What do you want out of life?"

Des contemplated the question further. He deliberated and then gave an answer which he knew was the only true answer he could give.

"I don't know, Mr Chen," said Des.

Chen smiled. He used his right index finger to brush his pencil sized moustache and whisper-thin beard that formed under the centre of his bottom lip. He then drew his left thumb and forefinger together to stroke the chin-stripe.

"You have come to me highly referenced, Mr Jamieson," said Chen. "Why would I put trust in someone who doesn't believe in their future?"

It was at that point Desmond Jamieson took William Chen's comment on the future seriously. He made further deliberations for a few moments and then spoke.

"Mr Chen, I am very good at what I do. I do it better than any other person you would dream of engaging."

"But to be truthful, I haven't put the energy I require into the future, because I have a past that I have trouble forgetting. But now it's time to move forwards. You have just reminded me of that fact and so I am here to tell you, I am here to make money," said Des as he stared directly into Chen's eyes.

"I have thoroughly checked your work history and indeed, your work ethics, so I assume the history you speak of, is of a personal nature," said Chen.

"Yes, it is."

"Then if that is the case and indeed, it is past history, then I will employ your services," proclaimed Chen.

"Why?" asked Des, intrigued with the whole process.

"Because I see you are an honest man and the job I have for you needs an honest man," Chen replied.

"Tell me more," Des said with interest sparked.

Chapter Nineteen

Des was to work on several assignments for Will Chen over the next two years.

Eighteen months in, Will asked Des to examine the entire Chen property portfolio. In reality, it was a case of multiple complex portfolios within one huge portfolio.

Will, of Chinese descent, spent most of his life in Singapore, using it as a base for many of his company's trade and property deals around the world.

It was the property deals that were causing Will most of his concerns. Des pored over the books and ledgers, studying every transaction over a three year period and something was not right.

There were properties listed in the tens of millions. Chen's company had either constructed them or had purchased, gutted and refurbished them for resale.

Des had been over the accounts three times and something was definitely wrong. There were three properties over a two and a half year period where the book values had changed between accounting periods, prior to their sale to another conglomerate. Technically, the figures showed that these properties would have been sold at a loss, but this was quite the opposite when reflected in the profit and loss statements.

Any auditor worth their salt would have picked this up, according to Des' thinking so he painstakingly went through all the accounts again. Same result. He then traced all of the corresponding bank statements which initially proved difficult as the transactions were dispersed over several different banks, three of them offshore.

After three days of careful auditing, Des came to one clear conclusion and one conclusion only. Someone was skimming the books, stealing from the overall proceeds from the property sales. He phoned Will Chen.

"Mr Chen, this is Desmond Jamieson," Des announced.

"Desmond, please call me Will," Chen replied, courteous as ever.

"Call me Des, then Will. I have a question to ask."

"Go on."

"I have found some discrepancies in your property portfolios relating to book values and the sales of three properties in particular."

"Meaning?"

"Based on monies spread over your various bank accounts, you would have made a loss, but in fact that is not the case."

"Desmond, I am not in the business of making losses."

"Precisely. This means that funds have been misappropriated."

"How much?"

"Somewhere in the vicinity of 30 million dollars, U.S."

"I feared this may be the case. That's one of the reasons I hired you."

"Who has been auditing your accounts?"

"Clarence Li."

"I think I need to talk to him."

"Meet me at my penthouse at seven o'clock tonight," said Chen, hanging up the phone.

***

Des took the lift to Chen's 54th floor penthouse, which occupied the entire top floor of Chen's luxury hotel. He had not been there before, as he had always met Chen either in the Raffles cafe or the revolving restaurant atop the Marriot to discuss business.

When the lift door opened, he was greeted not just by a formal manservant but the amazing layout of the apartment. He had been in smaller houses.

The suite started with a wide entrance hall leading to one step down to the right, where a marbled kitchen was situated, overlooking a further two steps down to a large open dining area.

The step immediately ahead led to an open living area, large enough to have a party for a hundred people, Des surmised. The step to the left opened up another sizable living area with a large study room at the rear. The study, which Des thought was a suite in itself, was enclosed by full length windows with most spectacular views across the city skyline and harbour. The sunset beyond was staining the skies orange and gold.

Similarly, the formal party room boasted incredible views as well as an open-air entertaining area and well-appointed garden. To the left, one would find five double bedrooms, all with full ensuite facilities.

Evidently, Chen had a liking for marble and lush carpets.

The butler showed Des into the office situated towards the rear of the penthouse, where Chen and another man awaited his arrival.

"You can leave now, Chi, thank you," said Chen, addressing the silent butler who quickly retreated.

Des heard the ping of the elevator, indicating that Chi had left the building or at least this very sophisticated penthouse level. Either way, there was only one way in or out of the apartment and that was via the lift as far as Des' observations went.

"Please, Desmond, join us and have a drink. I am having a whisky sour, what about you?"

"Just a scotch on the rocks please, Mr Chen," replied Des, still trying to take the surrounds of the 'Chen Chateau'.

"Coming right up. If I recall, you are either a Glenfiddich, single malt or a Chivas man, aren't you? And for goodness sake, call me Will. How many times do I have to ask?" said Chen, heading to the fully equipped bar, some metres to the left of the study area.

"Either is good enough for me, thanks Will," replied Des.

"Oh, my apologies," Chen said, as he put three blocks of ice into a crystal tumbler. "Forgive me please, let me make the appropriate introductions."

With a nod of the head, Chen, indicated the other man, while keeping a steady eye on Desmond.

"This is Clarence. Clarence, this is Desmond Jamieson. Do you need a top up of that martini, Clarence?" asked Will, every inch the polite host.

Clarence raised his hand and with a shake of his head, indicating no top up required. Clarence was much shorter than the other two men, with a round, full-moon face, with a full head of hair parted straight down the middle.

The two shook hands with cordial, *"Pleased to meet you"s* exchanged. Des instantly noticed Clarence's English was not as well pronounced as Chen's. A little more Cantonese, perhaps?

Des always considered Will Chen to be almost perfect in either language. Will had clearly been highly educated to ensure he was well conversant in any language he chose to do business in.

In the background, Will Chen was pouring scotch into the tumbler of ice. The ice crackled under the weight and high potency of the alcohol.

Des was feeling a little less comfortable, considering he potentially had damning evidence against this man he had never met before.

Will returned, handing the drink to Des and then motioned to them both to sit down in the leather armchairs in front of what was obviously Chen's desk. Des realised, as Chen sat behind the desk facing both of them, that there had to be a small raise or platform as suddenly Chen was a few inches higher than his meeting attendees. A very evident and strategic design element, Des contemplated.

"We should start with a toast," declared Will.

"What are we toasting?" asked Clarence.

Des remained quiet as he considered what was quickly appearing to be a game of chess, or in this case, Chinese checkers. He could feel the temperature rise. The mood in Chen was slightly changing. Was it the alcohol or a deliberate move to unsettle either Des or Clarence, or both?

Soon enough. Be patient, follow directions and play the game, Des.

"Oh Clarence, you know me. There's always something to celebrate," Chen quipped.

He held his glass aloft and clinked with the other two gentlemen and then he continued. He set the scene.

"Clarence, Desmond has been looking into some new property investments for me to consider."

Clarence was noticeably put out by this statement.

"That is what I have been doing for you Will, for the past seven years, so why involve this stranger all of a sudden?" blurted Clarence.

"Of course, Clarence. Yes, you have," Will replied, ever so calmly.

"But there are new opportunities all the time. I owe it to my company, my board of directors and of course, my family. You see that, don't you Clarence?"

"Let me worry about the new opportunities, Will." His round face creased with anxiety.

"It's not that simple anymore, Clarence. Desmond has also been doing some audit work for me in relation to our property portfolios."

Clarence squirmed a little, making a slight squeak against the soft leather upholstery.

"Desmond, I believe you have a few questions you would like to ask Clarence," said the ever-placid Chen.

"Sure, Will," said Des, taking up the lead.

"Clarence, I have looked at the books several times. I have audited the books and prospective values of all properties within all seven of the different property portfolios," said Des.

This time the squeak in the leather seating was far more audible.

"Then, Clarence, I have followed every transaction, from purchase, construction, development or refurbishment through to sale."

"Where are we going with this?" broke in Clarence, looking quite uneasy and wondering why he had declined the second martini, as he looked down at the two pale green olives at the bottom of his glass.

Des was on a roll now and was not prepared to break stride for the sake of a nervous Clarence.

"Clarence, there were three properties in the past two and a half years. They were undervalued on the accounts. As a matter of fact, the book values changed between reporting periods at a time of market prices rising," continued Des.

Clarence's skin colour was starting to turn. Ashen, is how Desmond would describe it.

"When this happens, Clarence, and those properties sell well above a falsely deflated book price but below actual market price, it means the company has still made a profit," Des continued.

"Well that's a good thing isn't it?" declared Clarence, his voice rising in pitch.

Chen remained still, his face emotionless.

"Indeed," continued Des, "It is always a good thing, making a profit, but not if the profit has been misappropriated compared with a devalued book amount."

"What's this got to do with me?" Clarence bleated, almost screeching, his chest feeling somewhat tighter.

"That's not the end of it, either," continued Des, "We then have the issue of when the monies from sales get spread across several bank accounts, two of which are not recognised by the Company."

"What are you trying to do?" shouted Clarence defensively. He leapt to his feet, abandoning the squeaky armchair and started to pace two steps back, two steps forward.

"Those two bank accounts are easily traceable," Des added softly, evenly. Clarence gripped the leather chair, his face twisted with guilt.

"You, Clarence, for whatever reason, misappropriated funds from the Company," Des concluded.

Job done, cheat exposed. Resignation or imprisonment? I don't care. That's up to the boss. All this and more raced through Desmond Jamieson's head.

Clarence was now wide-eyed, like a goldfish that has jumped out of its bowl. He was gasping, spitting out words, almost uncontrollably. He looked to Chen with eyes filled with desperation.

"Will, I have gambling debts, I'm sorry," he blurted.

Chen was now standing behind his desk, the palms of his hands firmly planted on the marble insert of its mahogany top. He stared implacably down at the miserable Clarence.

"We paid your debts, remember?" Chen lashed out.

"It won't happen again, please Will?" Clarence begged. His chubby hands clenched at the back of the armchair.

"You are right, Clarence. It can't; it will not happen again," Chen lowered his voice, calmness regained.

Des released a sigh of relief soundlessly; this was not going well.

Then it happened. So fast. No time to think, no time to intervene.

Will Chen opened his desk drawer, retrieved a revolver and shot Clarence in the heart, point blank.

Clarence fell forward, slumped over the back of the leather armchair that only moments before, he had squirmed in.

Desmond Jamieson's mouth was agape, his finger touching the side of his right cheek, where blood spatter stained his face. Across the chest and shoulder of his latest Fletcher Jones suit, the full cotton blend became blotting paper as the drops of crimson sank in. His eyes were wide as the shock rocked him.

"Desmond, are you alright?" asked Chen, as Des saw the world spinning before his eyes.

"Are you alright, Desmond?" asked Chen, this time more assertively.

It was Chen's cool, monotone voice that brought Des back to reality or was it reality? It felt like a dream or nightmare just waiting for him to wake up.

"For Christ's sake, Will, what the fuck have you done?" shouted Des, as he broke out of the trance.

"Des, Des, look at me. This had to happen," Chen spoke insistently, his voice calm and measured.

"I can't be a part of murder, Chen," Des said angrily.

"You are right, and you will not be."

"No fucking way; this is fucking murder. We have to call the police!"

"Settle, Desmond," Chen was authoritative. Des took a deep, cold breath.

"How does that work, I'm a witness, or do you plan to kill me also?" Des became more agitated.

"Relax, Des. You are, and I repeat, you are a faithful consultant to my business, and I am your ever-faithful client, but you must understand, I cannot let my employees steal from the Company, Des." Will put the gun back into the drawer and closed it with a firm click.

"But why did you have to kill him?"

"He didn't just steal from the Company, Desmond. He stole from me while lying to my face, and worse, he has stolen from our family honour."

Des' head was still spinning, he thought he might vomit, but he took a deep breath as Chen's last words sank in.

"What do you mean, family honour?" asked Des.

"Clarence is, *was*, my brother-in-law."

"Oh my God," said Des, "We are both going to prison and what of your sister?"

"He has not been treating my sister well," remarked Chen coldly. "He has been abusive. She will move on."

Chen returned to the bar and filled two more glasses with scotch on the rocks. Des, hearing that familiar crackling sound, looked up from the chair he had seemingly been affixed to for the past half hour.

Time flies when you are having fun or witnessing a murder, thought Des in shock. An out of body experience, he was observing himself as if in a mirror. He forced his trembling hands to become still by sheer willpower.

Accepting the glass from Chen, he took an initial large gulp, followed by a shorter gulp. The glass was almost empty and Chen handed the second glass to the shaken, pale Jamieson. From the corner of his eye, he noticed Clarence's overturned martini glass on the floor, the two pale green olives lying slug-like and abandoned on the wet carpet.

Another sip and instead of heading to inebriation, his mind seemed suddenly clearer. Stress dissipated. What had he said to himself, some forty minutes ago?

Job done, cheat exposed. Resignation or imprisonment? I don't care. That's up to the boss.

Now he was either an accomplice or a witness. Thoughts charged through his mind as he weighed up his options. A witness, yes, but the testimony of a foreigner from Australia who has never been in the 54th floor penthouse of one of the most famous hotels in Singapore, might not ever be considered. Will Chen, the owner of the hotel, might have more to say. Wield more influence.

Suddenly, Des was alert, as panic regarding his circumstances now replaced the preceding shock.

"I have to get out of here, Will, before someone comes. Please."

"Relax, all is taken care of," reassured Will, in even, almost nonchalant tones.

"What now, Will?"

Desmond's fists were closed tightly, his knuckles turning white. He wanted to punch Will or throw the blood-splattered chair he was sitting on through the window. Of course, the other chair remained occupied with the silent corpse slumped over it.

"I want you to continue to work for me Desmond," said Chen.

"Not sure about that; I think my job here is done," said Des with contempt in his voice as he swallowed hard and desperately tried to keep in control of himself.

"Just the beginning. We have many more businesses to build or rebuild. I need the sharpness of your mind and your honesty." Chen said briskly.

Chen saw the hesitation in Des' eyes and understood him totally.

"Des, it is up to you. You will have other clients, I am sure, but I need a point guard. I think that's what Westerners call it, don't they? I need a minder. Too many rely on me. Family, the Company, a thousand or so employees. I work hard, Des but I do so with honour."

"Is murder honourable?"

"In this case, I believe so," said Chen, looking at the slumped and lifeless body of his brother-in-law.

"What happens now?" asked Des, almost resigned to the creeping sense of numbness beyond the shock.

"You will exit via the second lift, it's at the back of the wardrobe in the master suite. Chi will be in the basement waiting for you with a car. Go to your hotel and pack. Shower. Place all your current clothing in the hotel laundry bag and return to your hotel's basement car park."

"I still have to check out and pay the account."

"Already taken care of, Desmond. Give the laundry bag to Chi. He will drive you to the airport. Take a few weeks off in the Bahamas. I particularly like the Ocean Club; I think you will find it an excellent choice. All tickets and visas are taken care of."

"Then what?" Desmond's mind was spinning as he tried to take it all in.

"Return to Australia, and set up your business as you always suggested you would. You are free, free from all of this."

"How can I be free, if I am a witness?"

"A witness to what, Desmond Jamieson?"

Des grimaced but realised there wasn't a lot of choice. He needed to leave the building, the country, if he wanted to get clear of this disaster.

"There will be one million US dollars in your bank account by the morning and subsequently every year, whilst you and I, of course, live," Chen smiled.

"Are you buying me off?" Des was staggered.

"Not at all, Desmond. You are a man I trust. I will pay you for any work you do for me across the globe. The one million US dollars is a mere bonus, which I suspect you will earn over and over, and if it doesn't work out, we shake hands and say goodbye." He held out his hand, business concluded.

Des shook hands with Will, too stunned to see the blood on his fingers transferring to Will's smooth hand. But then Will drew him close into a hug and whispered, *"Do not lose sleep over matters of family honour."*

Des was ushered to the secret second lift, leaving the bloody scene behind him. He had no doubt all traces of it would soon be erased.

***

Part Four

The life and times
of Lauren Black

*"Yesterday is gone. Tomorrow has not yet come. We
have only today. Let us begin."*

Mother Teresa

Chapter Twenty

Lauren had been brought up in a most loving home. Her mother Caitlin was not doting as such, but challenging. Lauren was challenged in every aspect to what decisions she made.

"I don't care what you do, young lady, as long as you have the heart to do it," was her mother's demand.

Lauren reflected on those words over and over in her mind and grew up with the belief the words intended to etch into her persona.

There wasn't a lot of money on hand when she was young. Her father had simply left when she was a baby, was what she was told. She had no memory of her father, so she considered herself abandoned and therefore never paid it too much mind until she reached eight years of age, and then it played on her mind a lot.

She had friends who had parents, two of them. Even if they were divorced, except for the odd one, as she considered herself to be, there was a father.

In the past, her mother had dismissed it with very little explanation. Her curiosity and thoughts of a father that had abandoned her caused anxiety over not being wanted or loved.

She started to become quiet and was not connecting with her schoolwork or her friends. Her mother started to worry so one day Caitlin decided to get to the bottom of her daughter's withdrawal and decided to seek professional counselling, regardless of the cost.

Before doing so, Caitlin sat down with her daughter and expressed her love and concerns.

"Is there anything you want to talk about, Lauren? You've been so quiet and sad lately," her mother asked, uncertain of her approach and unsure of what to do with any response.

To Lauren's credit, she proved to be more intuitive than her mother gave credit for an eight-year-old. She shrugged her skinny young shoulders.

"I just want to know the truth. Did my daddy not like me?"

Caitlin was almost aghast but took a deep breath and said that her father had died before she was born.

"Why didn't you tell me?" little Lauren sobbed.

"I'm sorry, Lorrie, I was wrong not to do so but it's hard because he was a good man."

"How did he die?" asked Lauren through her tears. She was relieved to hear that it was not about her; it was not about a monster father who had been an abusive arsehole, as was the case with her friend Mia.

Caitlin breathed in, closing her eyes with the very thought of her dead partner and simply replied,

"Heart disease, he died with a heart disease at a young age and let me tell you, my beautiful child, he would have loved you to bits."

Lauren finally gave a grimace that could be taken as the slightest of smiles. The tears were drying on her cheeks as Caitlin reached out and hugged her daughter, realising that the truth for her daughter alleviated her anxiety.

"Any more questions?" asked Caitlin.

"A couple but I don't want it to upset you," her child replied. Caitlin was again reminded of her daughter's intuition and maturity.

"What was my father's name?"

"His name was, and you will possibly laugh at this, his name was Oliver, Oliver Black."

"Oliver, like 'Oliver Twist', the musical?"

"Yes, Oliver, it's indeed an old-fashioned name but like all names, they come back into fashion. Do you know, I think Lauren is an even older name in history than Oliver so never judge a name."

"I never do, after all where does Mia come from? And don't you always say don't judge a book by its cover?"

"Yes, I do, and that wise saying is older than all of our ages put together."

Caitlin started to breathe a little easier, perhaps because she had finally released past tensions. Her personal life was now on show.

"And your other questions?" asked Caitlin, knowing there was more to come.

"What about grandparents, don't I have some of them, too?"

"Sadly, my love, they are also long gone."

"What was my daddy like?"

"He was a wonderful person."

"What made him wonderful?"

"He had the ability to make everyone around him feel happy, including me."

"Are you sad too, that he is not here?"

"Sometimes babe, but he died so long ago that I decided to focus on us and while he may have been a great dad, I know he would have wanted the best for you."

The fact that there were no photos of her father or grandparents never dawned on her at that stage. She just took it in and accepted it as it was. While she thought it would have been so much better to have a father or even a grandfather or grandmother, this was her life. Just her mother and her.

***

Lauren quickly grew and left the remains of her dead father within her mother's memories. It was no longer a constant anguishing question in her mind. When she was asked, she simply said her father died when she was very young.

By the time she entered high school, those dimensions changed. Those kids without two parents seemed to be cruelly treated by the bullies of this world. Ironically, many of the bullies were from a single parent or abusive parent upbringing.

Lauren or 'Lorrie' as her mother endearingly called her, found a way to fight back against the bullies. She grew in height and literally ran rings around her competitors, whether it was on a netball, basketball or tennis court. Her speed around a netball court was simply staggering.

Her stature continued to grow and the so-called gangs began circling some of her shorter friends. One day, when one attempted to start a fight with a slap, Lauren slapped back with a vengeance. Lauren was suspended for three weeks for breaking the other girl's nose, but was greeted with admiration from her underling friends, her mother and even a secret, warm smile from the headmistress.

Lauren left high school with very little ambition. She had scant money in her pocket, other than earning some income from the local McDonalds' drive-through and no interest in being a corporate high-flier. Her experience with high school bullies, however, gave her a thirst for helping others.

Her marks had amazingly allowed her into university for a social science and psychology course. She shrugged her shoulders until she attended her first lecture which commanded her attention for the first time since fourth grade maths.

A passion was stirred. Lauren was alive and for the first time could not dream of anything else but to make a difference.

That changed when she met the man she would ultimately fall in love with and marry at the age of twenty-six.

Chapter Twenty-one

The park where Senior Constable Michael Fagan had agreed to rendezvous with Jack Bissen was a small reserve in North Fitzroy. It consisted of some patchy grass, a disused children's slide and swing, a toilet block covered with graffiti, and a few overarching gum trees that had evidently resisted the temptation to curl up and die amongst the numerous expended syringes strewn beneath.

Bissen, as toey as ever, had been waiting impatiently for more than an hour when the Senior Constable walked up and landed a punch to Bissen's midsection. Bissen doubled over in pain, winded by the force of the punch.

"What the fuck did you do that for?" wheezed the almost breathless Bissen.

"In case someone's watching," replied Fagan casually.

Bissen looked around and knew Fagan was talking bullshit, with no one to be seen. Only the druggies came to this park these days and generally in the late twilight hours, not in the middle of the day as it was now.

Fagan watched Bissen's eyes dart around the perimeter of the reserve and just smiled. To him, Bissen was low-life scum that needed more than a jab to the guts.

"Anyway, you have something for me Jacky boy?" rasped Fagan.

Still attempting to breathe normally, Bissen reached inside his denim jacket and retrieved the two hundred dollars and handed it cautiously to the police officer.

"Hmm, not much considering what you took from those kids," said Fagan.

"Yes, that's right Jacky boy, they came into the station and just lucky, I happened to be there to ensure their complaint was filed. Now, you got something else for me?"

"I gotta fucking live, don't I?" stammered Bissen.

"Sure you do Jacky boy, but you know what I mean."

With that, Bissen again reached inside his jacket and resentfully handed over a small plastic bag filled with white powder to Fagan.

"You see, that's more like it. No need to hold back now, is there? And next time you decide to make a hit on my turf, you may want to think about the percentages; you understand?"

Bissen nodded. Fagan reached forward and gave him a light slap to the side of his face, turned and walked away.

Bissen cursed under his breath but was happy that all had been settled for the day and he could move on. He tapped his jacket above the pocket where plenty more of the white stuff awaited him, along with the cash. Instead of dwelling on the short ordeal with Fagan, he was feeling quite good about himself, particularly knowing he had several hundred dollars still in his pocket – *time to celebrate a little.*

***

Chapter Twenty-two

Lauren hadn't considered herself to be any sort of beauty queen, although there had been a few boys wanting to date her when she was in university. That in itself, had been unfamiliar territory as no boys had paid any attention to her in high school.

Her first meaningful relationship and subsequent sexual encounter was with a nineteen year old boy by the name of Robert Channing.

Robert was in the same psychology behavioural science class as Lauren and was struggling with the course material. He had watched Lauren from a distance and had plucked up the courage to sit down in the cafeteria with her one lunchtime.

"Hi, I'm Robert," he awkwardly said as he sat down.

"Hi, I'm Lauren" she replied, offering a hand to shake which he readily accepted but in a loose, trembling way.

"I'm in your psychology behavioural science class."

"Yes, I know."

Robert was either impressed or amazed that she even knew he was in the same class, as he blushed at her response.

They then shared small chat. Where they came from, what schools they attended, what they wanted to do post university and so forth.

They met each day for lunch at the same table at the same cafeteria for the next two weeks and mainly discussed the course material. Robert was well out of his depth in these conversations which Lauren quickly recognised, but didn't tell him so. In reality, she became somewhat of a mentor as she provided a different perspective to his on many occasions.

Robert finally got the nerve to ask Lauren out for a drink one Friday night. Although she did not see herself as that attractive, she also considered Robert to be no rock star but thought having a drink or two would do no harm. At the same time, Robert viewed Lauren as nothing less than stunning and he knew that many of his fellow students were of the same opinion.

At the time, Lauren was sharing a two-bedroom flat with another student, Isabel Morrison, who was not taking the same course but studying geology instead.

Isabel aka Issie, was a good student with very plain appearance. However, Isabel knew how to party and how to party hard. Very often, she would come home with a boy while Lauren was studying, and without any notice. The dull thud on the thin wall that separated the two girls' bedrooms was constant and Lauren had often thought of moving Izzie's bedhead a little further from the wall.

With Issie, it never seemed to be the same man coming home with her, although the constant rhythmic thumping on the wall was the same, even if the time span was sometimes shorter than others.

Lauren wondered what her magic secret was and how she attracted so many boys. On asking, Isabel's reply was that she was just herself and didn't allow any inhibitions to get in the way.

"You need to get with it, Lauren," Issie said.

"It's not me," said Lauren.

"Then that's your loss but that will change." Issie grinned.

"Maybe."

"When it does, just make sure they have a condom. I don't bring anyone home without one," she counselled.

Lauren was nineteen. She thought she was behind the game. Most of her high school girlfriends had lost their virginity by the time they were sixteen, some even earlier. Was she a late bloomer? Maybe she would never blossom, she thought.

So on a Friday night after more than a couple of drinks, in a semi-drunk state, Lauren brought Robert back to the flat. Robert was also inebriated but Lauren still had Izzie's words in her head, so regardless of their lack of sobriety she pushed him into a supermarket to purchase the required protection.

That night, whilst virginity was lost, was not spectacular in Lauren's view. The only common factor was that the wall-thumping had an echo.

Lauren shunted Robert out the door the next morning and turned around to see a bleary-eyed Issie.

"So?" Isabel asked eagerly, ready for all of the details.

"I am not going to grace you with any details, Issie. Suffice to say, I am going to be a little more choosy in the future," said Lauren, sighing.

Robert and Lauren never dated again although there was the odd lunch in the cafeteria and a casual drink. Romance dies as quickly as it emerges, Lauren thought initially, but perhaps it was a case of lust and not so much the romance factor. Lauren surmised, somewhat enviously, that Issie was a lust queen.

Lauren was to also have a number of lustful moments, including some short-lived relationships during those later university days.

When she graduated, there was great relief and much to celebrate. Her mother, Caitlin, was front and centre in the auditorium and no one could have been prouder of a daughter than Caitlin was.

For Caitlin, she thought her daughter having an education would provide life opportunities that she never had. For Lauren, it was a little scary. An education was one thing, having a job and an opportunity out in the world was another.

***

During her final three years of study, Lauren had performed placement work in three different settings. The first was with a psychology consultancy bureau where she was allowed, based on client acceptance, to sit in on sessions and take notes.

The reality of this experience did not stretch too much imagination for Lauren. They were the 'tame and safe' cases, although one did spark her attention.

The client, a woman by the name of Beatrice Marlowe, talked of a recurring dream where she was being stabbed several times but then went swimming, the blood spurting out like the exhale of a sperm whale. She then laughed at the absurdity of the dream after telling her story.

Beatrice was living in an abusive co-dependent relationship with a man called Clive. The abuse came in two forms, mainly mental abuse where Beatrice was made to feel worthless as she supposedly didn't meet his needs and then the *occasional* physical abuse.

Lauren thought *occasional* in terms of abuse was once too many. Beatrice's psychologist and Lauren's work placement supervisor, Dr Matthias Wilson, encouraged Beatrice to make changes to her life, break the cycle and get out of the relationship.

Lauren sat through consecutive sessions with Beatrice over three weeks and nothing changed except the stabbings got worse, the swimming got longer, as if Beatrice was swimming the English Channel, and the blood didn't spurt in geyser fashion. The laughter at the end of her descriptions diminished in tear-filled eyes.

After the third appointment and Beatrice's departure from the clinic, Dr Matthias Wilson turned to Lauren to test her views.

"So, what do you think is happening for Beatrice, Lauren?" he asked.

Lauren pondered for a moment and considered her response.

"Beatrice has shifted," said Lauren.

"Yes," agreed Wilson, almost in a dull, frustrated way as if to say, *that's fucking obvious.*

"I think Beatrice is in danger," said Lauren.

"Why do you say that?"

"She's no longer dying from the stabbings in her dreams. In fact, she is swimming without pain and yet, she is remorseful at the end."

Matthias Wilson looked at Lauren, not in a manner of acknowledging her intuition, but with the chilling realisation of the fact that this student had seen more than he had.

"So what do you think the outcome will be?" he asked.

"Beatrice is a danger to herself, but she is a danger to Clive first and foremost."

Matthias then became sceptical and scoffed at Lauren's analysis.

"You can't jump to conclusions so far and so remote from the fact that Beatrice is insecure, living in a co-dependent relationship; co-dependent to the point that she thrives on it," he said.

Lauren's face reddened with embarrassment. She realised she had been outspoken with no credentials other than her gut feel. She doubted everything at that point, questioned why she was undertaking the studies of her choice and all but made up her mind to pull the pin on the outplacement work.

When she returned to the agency the next morning to advise Dr Wilson of her decision, she entered his office to find Matthias behind his desk with his head in his hands. He looked up at Lauren, his face ashen.

"I had a phone call this morning," he said, "from the police."

A chill gripped Lauren's heart, but she didn't say anything, just waited for her supervisor to continue.

"Beatrice Marlowe is dead. She weighed herself down with a sack of bricks and she was found in her backyard swimming pool."

"That's terrible," blurted Lauren, tears springing to her eyes.

"There's more… Clive, her partner, was found in the bath… he had been stabbed thirteen times."

Lauren's second work placement was as a drug and alcohol counsellor at an adolescent welfare centre. While the work was challenging, she shone.

Here, there were teenagers who had been left to fend for themselves and were often living in the streets. Drugs were too plentiful, as was the level of addiction. Teenagers having sex, or giving head jobs, to predatory adults for a pittance, just enough to support their addictions, was rife.

Her ability to take these youngsters, and listen, truly listen to their stories, find new accommodation, garner fostering arrangements and so much more was truly remarkable. Lauren's passion for her work was well commended by the end of her three month tenure, but while she was passionate about the work, she was not convinced this was her calling.

Lauren's final work placement assignment was in her last year of studies. She was twenty-five years of age and still hadn't worked out what she wanted to do for a career.

Her final work-study placement was what she considered almost an insult. She was appointed to the Northern Hospital in Windsor where her job was merely to talk to patients, pre or post operations, check on their spirits and talk to them if they were feeling down, analyse their temperament and advise if any further counselling may be required.

***

Chapter Twenty-three

56 Earl Street in West Kingston was a mere fifteen minute walk from City General Hospital but this evening, the walk seemed to be considerably longer for Lauren. She had the world on her shoulders, thinking of her conversation with Amelia Schwartz and her new patient, Des Jamieson.

Before getting home, she would have to stop by 51 Earl Street, where her neighbour and close friend Alison Fischer was looking after her daughter, Eileen.

Alison verged on being a hypochondriac, with a multitude of problems, none of which were real. However, once you got Alison off the central subject of herself, she was actually a very good listener and a true friend to Lauren.

That made Alison unique to say the least.

It was already 6.30 pm by the time Lauren got to Alison's house. She walked in, not bothering to ring the doorbell, as this was the accepted norm.

Alison, with her naturally wavy red hair, raised one hand and pointed towards the refrigerator while the other hand held the phone pressed to her ear. Lauren knew the cue, going to the cabinet and retrieving two wine glasses.

She opened the fridge to extract a bottle of sauvignon blanc and poured two generous glasses. Before even sipping, she walked into the family room, where both Eileen and Tim were engaged in an episode of Buffy on Foxtel.

"Hey, there," she said.

"Hi mum," said Eileen, with barely a glance toward her mother.

"All good?"

"Yep, Tim's been a pain but nothing out of the ordinary."

"Bugger off, Eils," was Tim's friendly retort to his friend. With that, Lauren smiled and returned to the kitchen, where Alison was concluding her conversation.

The two women looked at each other, shrugged shoulders, clinked glasses and took their first sip of wine.

"So who were you on the phone to?" asked Lauren.

"James," Alison replied sheepishly.

"James? You mean your beloved ex, James?"

"Yeah, OK, ex-James but let's not go there."

"Go where?" Lauren teased innocently.

"I am telling you, we are not going there. Just leave it alone," Alison took an extra-large sip of her wine. Actually, more of a gulp than a sip.

"OK, that's fine. So, just exactly how is James?"

"Bitch!"

They both laughed, knowing very well that James was still a major player in Alison's life. They occasionally still slept together but had no plans for a full recommitment of their wedding vows of fifteen years ago.

Lauren considered this to be a perfect arrangement and was a little envious of the fact.

James was a reporter for the popular morning to midday talkback radio program on 3FZ. He was considered to be the thought provocateur on the station with all the up to date information. Generally he was spot on.

"So, what about you?" asked the inquisitive Alison.

"So, so."

"Ah, yep – more info, please?"

"I don't know. I have a new patient and I haven't had time to scratch my fanny to understand who he is."

"So?"

"So, I think he is important."

"You tell me they are all important."

"No, I mean *really* important. The boss certainly thinks so."

"Tell me more."

"No, you know I can't, but I don't even know yet."

"What do you mean? How old is he? You haven't fallen for a patient have you?"

"No, fuck off. He's sixty-eight years old, for God's sake! Right now, he's a mystery, and I for the love and life of me can't think why."

That closed the conversation and a second glass was poured.

***

By the time she got Eileen home at 9.30, Lauren was very weary, as was her daughter, who promptly brushed her teeth and went to bed.

They had shared a good helping of spaghetti bolognaise at her friend's house and well and truly finished the second bottle of wine plus one more glass each from a third bottle. At that stage, Lauren knew it was time to go home.

She and Alison had talked rubbish for three hours. They had moved off the subject of Lauren's patients, particularly the new and right now, in Lauren's mind, mysterious Des Jamieson.

There had been some further chat about Alison's ex, James, which just led to hushed chuckles, particularly so when Tim from the next room had called out to ask what they were talking about.

James picked Tim up every second weekend to spend time together but the rekindled almost teen-like affair between his mother and father was, to the best of Alison's belief, a total secret. If Tim did know, he had been very tight-lipped about it.

Lauren thought that Tim was the spitting image of his father; dimples indented on both cheeks with every smile.

Crystal blue eyes that would definitely be a winner with the girls when he grew up.

Lauren thought again how perfect it was for the two lovers but not a genuine solution for the long term. She speculated about the eventual regathering of the family and the effect it could have on young Tim.

She quietly stepped into Eileen's bedroom to say goodnight, only to find her daughter already asleep. As tired as she felt, she was still very much alert.

She did take some solace knowing that tomorrow was Saturday and she didn't have to go to work. A sleep-in at last, she thought. Perhaps a supermarket shop, then take Eileen to netball and watch her lose.

The whole team was a disaster; they hadn't won a game all season and yet, she was proud to sit there knowing Eileen ran around and did her best. In her mind, she was the best player on the court.

Yes, Saturday and no work. She went to the hall cupboard. It was the linen and liquor cupboard, combined. Amongst that which is ironed is that which can iron you out, she always quipped.

She pulled out the bottle of brandy, went to the kitchen and held a glass to the refrigerator dispenser, which generously emptied three ice cubes, to which she added some dry ginger. Filling the remainder of the glass with brandy, she sipped and sighed and thought all was good.

Yet, as she went to sit on her favourite armchair in her living room, she knew something was still amiss. She had a new patient and Des Jamieson was clearly not going to exit her mind.

Well here's to you Des Jamieson, let's find out who you really are.

Retreating to the corner of the living room, also known as her study, Lauren started up her home computer and the low buzz it made was a reminder that after five years, it needed replacing.

She rubbed her weary eyes and thought what a waste of time this was going to be but as the Windows page opened with Google, she said to herself, *Why not?*

She was amazed after tapping in the name, *Desmond Jamieson.* Page after page of links sprang to life. She quickly scanned and dismissed a myriad of Des and Desmond Jamiesons that could not be her new patient, either by age or currency.

Some entries were internationals and she disregarded the links from Scotland, Ireland and the UK for the time being. She also noted a link that related to Singapore and another in Indonesia.

However, her initial focus was on the Australian content, starting with the most recent entries. The first was only three months ago. July. In fact there were numerous mentions in July, and if this was her Des Jamieson, as well could be the case, she surmised that July may well have been just before he had succumbed to his illness.

Less than three months ago her patient was still an active member on a number of organisations' board of directors. These positions varied considerably across different industry sectors.

He was the deputy chair to the National Cancer Federation, chair of the Australian Business Industry Commission, director of the Business Advisory Group to Government, convener of the Children's Cancer Outreach Organisation - the list went on and on. She was now convinced this was indeed *her* Des Jamieson.

Lauren did not choose to drill down into the Google entries, not yet at least. At this time of the night, she just wanted a feel for the subject. Her patient.

The ice in her brandy tumbler had either shrunk and the alcohol equally evaporated, or she needed a refill. She chose the latter, but thought it smart to dilute the potency with some extra dry ginger ale. Satisfied with convincing herself that some level of soberness remained, she then looked a little closer into the Internet exposure of her patient.

One thing to be said about the month of July for Des Jamieson, it was extremely busy. Perhaps not in a good way, but busy all the same.

Media articles scrolled on the screen before her, one after the other. How was it she didn't know him? Obviously, they travelled in different circles. That wasn't surprising to her. She rarely caught the news and what she caught when she did, never pleased her.

Many of the reports cited his resignation from one board or another, or several. All stated his departure was for 'personal family' reasons.

Family. Lauren hadn't had the opportunity to explore the subject with her patient, but she was hopeful that if the reports were accurate, then there would be a spouse or children, a brother or a sister that could be called upon to be part of the process.

Hitting the keyboard, she added some additional wording to Des Jamieson in her search bar. Personal. Family. The dull whir of her hard drive ended but no new entries appeared.

She added the word *wife*. The computer made a grinding noise as if it was too tired to even try, but a few seconds later, up came an additional entry. No, entries after entries. More and more.

One link that caught her eye related to many years prior; an article relating to someone by the name of Janice Lee, the wife of Desmond Jamieson. The article read more like an obituary.

As she perused the article, she learned that *Ms Janice Lee, born in 1964 died after a short and tragic illness. We have no other information in relation to her illness, but she had been married to Mr Desmond Jamieson for less than a year. Mr Jamieson is a successful businessman, consulting to some of the wealthiest businesses across south east Asia.*

Mr Jamieson was not available for comment but his client and most notable friend, Mr William Chen of the Xiaou conglomerate in Singapore, placed the following statement of respect in the Today newspaper: We are very saddened by the loss and we convey our deepest condolences to our friend, Mr Desmond Jamieson.

Then the search engine cranked up more names. *Vivian Jamieson claims ten million dollars in divorce suit against business leader Desmond Jamieson.*

The story that unfolded on the screen before her stated that Vivian, Desmond's second wife had settled their divorce at a significant sum. The photos of Vivian portrayed an attractive and slim body with pitch black hair, long thin nose and rosy cheeks.

She was definitely a beauty, model material thought Lauren, and would have been much younger than Des when the divorce took place. Lauren did the calculations. This divorce would have been 15 years after the death of his first wife, Janice Lee Jamieson.

What stunned Lauren was the magnitude of the divorce settlement; ten million dollars. *Christ, who has that sort of money!* Obviously, Des Jamieson, or at least, he did at the time.

But there was a more important clue in this story. Vivian not only took control of a house and ten million dollars but also her eight-year-old daughter, Fiona Alice Jamieson.

While it was a huge financial loss, her patient might still want to connect with his step-daughter.

Chapter Twenty-four

Mum. Mum, Mum.

Finally the words penetrated, and Lauren moved reluctantly under the doona, then cranked one eye open, a small groan and she was looking up at her daughter. Why was she dressed in her netball gear?

"Mum, we have to go in half an hour," said Eileen, at which Lauren sat up straight, looked at her alarm clock and said, "Shit."

It is Saturday, pull yourself together, Lauren.

"It's OK Eileen, plenty of time. I am entitled to a small sleep-in, aren't I?" she pleaded, not wanting to sound harsh.

"Sure, just wanted to know you were going to wake up at some stage today," said Eileen. *Her daughter could be quite a smart-arse at times.*

Lauren had finally gone to bed with the thoughts of Des Jamieson, his wives and finally a step-daughter. These would all be subjects of conversation she would have with her patient – according to Amelia Schwartz, the most important patient since the world began.

The half bottle of brandy and what was left of the dry ginger had somehow descended into a mire of thoughts mixed with a rush of adrenalin. It had been like entering a detective mystery where only some of the pieces of the puzzle had been revealed.

Perhaps Amelia Schwartz was right, and her gut feel about this patient being a potential life changer was correct. She just could not articulate the instinct to her friend, Alison. She was keen to know more, so much more.

After the quickest shower and even quicker make-up placement in her memory, Lauren was in the car with her daughter heading to yet another netball travesty. A record of twenty minutes and, enough time for a drive-through at McDonalds for an egg and bacon muffin.

"I'm impressed mum," said Eileen as she bit into her muffin.

Lauren just smiled, her head slightly pounding. The first bite of the junk food, which she would normally detest, tasted really, really good.

They arrived at the netball court, an outside venue at a council reserve which consisted of several courts, all active with competition. There had been many a time that Lauren had selfishly prayed for rain and while she felt guilty in those thoughts, there was no answer to the prayer today. The clear blue skies prevailed, and she was there as steadfast as ever, to cheer her daughter on, regardless of the result.

But today was different somehow. Firstly, as Lauren drove into the car park, she noticed a familiar vehicle; her mother's. Her mother seldom came to the games but was always the first on the phone on a game day evening to see how her granddaughter and the team had gone.

Secondly, as Eileen raced out to the court with her team and coach, Eileen had the GA singlet draped over her. This indeed was a big change. Eileen had been playing defence all season with mixed results and now she had been switched to Goal Attack position. *Wow,* thought Lauren.

Lauren walked up to her mother and gave her the traditional hug and kiss while watching the teenage girls warm up, throwing the ball in criss-cross fashion to each other.

"Gosh, Mum, nice to see you here but I wasn't expecting you," said Lauren.

"Well, I keep wanting to come and there's always something popping up, you know what I mean," said her mother.

"Yeah, I know what you mean." She shoved her hands deep into her parka pockets, savouring the warmth.

Lauren didn't in fact know what her mother meant, nor did she ever know what *something popping up* entailed.

"So how is work going, Lorrie?' asked her mother.

"All good," replied Lauren but midstream her mobile phone pinged, and she reflexively looked at the text message.

"Sorry, I need to call work." Lauren walked away and hit autodial for the hospital ward.

"Cambria unit," was the hoarse and almost gruff response once connected. Lauren recognised the voice of Libby Andersen.

"Libby, this is Lauren, what's the go?"

"Oh, hi Lauren," Libby's voice magically softened.

Lauren couldn't help but think that the gruffness was just a defence mechanism and Libby was not comfortable with handling potential incoming calls from the family members of the patients in the ward.

"It's about Noela Henderson," said Libby.

"Go on Libby, I'm listening," Lauren replied.

"According to Shelley at PalCare, you had marked the file to be notified."

"Yes, I promised the family, so I guess Noela has passed?"

"Yes and Shelley has the family scheduled to be coming in at four this afternoon. She wants to know if you can make it."

Lauren gave a deep sigh and gave the affirmative that she would be there.

"While I have you, Libby, any update on my current load?"

Libby looked up and down on the status sheet.

"Not much to report, other than Desmond Jamieson."

"And..?"

"He woke at 11pm last night and started to make phone calls."

"Oh. Has he asked for anything?"

"No, hasn't buzzed or anything but I know he has gotten up and walked to the toilet with the drip."

"Thanks Libby, catch you later," Lauren ended the call.

"Not today, you won't," Libby replied, "I'm due to go off in five minutes. See you next week."

He's making calls at 11pm at night; who does that? Was he calling family, his step-daughter, ex-wife? What was her name? Vivian, yes Vivian. Surely not, not after losing his fortune to her.

The thoughts kept coming as she walked back to courtside where the game had just started.

Her mother was already engrossed in the game as she stood next to her.

"Everything all right, love?" asked Caitlin.

"All good but I'll have to call in to work on the way home. Would you mind if Eileen went with you for a couple of hours?" said Lauren.

"Not a problem at all, but it is your day off, isn't it?"

"Yes, it's a patient that's passed, and I promised the family that when the time came I would meet with them one last time."

"I see," said her mother and then, "Look Lorrie, Eileen has the ball!"

Eileen indeed had the ball and almost nonchalantly, tossed it straight through the goal ring. Lauren gave the loudest cheer imaginable, at which Eileen turned and gave a radiant smile.

Eileen was to score two more goals, but the team did not win, going down by a single goal but she was enjoying the happiest moment of her short netball career. She didn't even wince when her mother told her that she had to go to work for a little while and besides, she loved spending time with her grandmother.

Chapter Twenty-five

When Lauren entered the PalCare wing of City General, she did so with mixed thoughts and emotions.

PalCare was not a happy place and fortunately Lauren only went there to either say goodbye or to help the family with closure. Most of her work was generally complete before the patient went to PalCare.

At PalCare, some lasted hours, some days and some a week or two at the best. Life had escaped them before they knew it and morphine was generally their opportunity to catch up. They went to sleep peacefully and never woke up.

Shelley greeted her at the reception desk.

"Nice to see you Lauren," said Shelley.

"You too Shelley, where am I going?" said Lauren.

"Ward 15."

"You mean the family is still with..."

"Yep, they are still by her bedside and we need to get things moving, if you know what I mean."

"Sure, let's see what I can do," said Lauren as she walked down the west wing of the floor. *Why the hell would they want to stay this amount of time by a corpse?*

When she entered ward 15, she was quite taken aback. Noela was not there; she had been removed but her family was there waiting. She instantly recognised Noela's daughter, Mary, a frequent visitor, and smiled.

Mary stepped up and gave Lauren a hug and a kiss to her cheek and whispered, "Thank you." She then introduced her husband Trevor and her two children, Neville and Nancy.

After the greetings and some small chat with Lauren giving her condolences, Trevor walked to the table at the side of the empty hospital bed where five glasses and a bottle of Dom Perignon rested in an ice bucket. He quickly curled the foil and popped the cork as if he had done this many times before.

"What is this?" asked Lauren, a little bemused by the whole affair.

"It's a thank you, Lauren, and a celebration of mum's life at the same time," said Mary.

"No need for the thanks or recognition. It's my job after all," said Lauren.

"But you do it to perfection and mum said you were a god-send and I saw that you were."

"Well, then cheers and here's to Noela," conceded Lauren, a little embarrassed as they all clinked their glasses.

Lauren left the ward and PalCare feeling much brighter. It had been a great day after all, regardless of the sluggish start. It had been great with Eileen starring on the netball court and now accolades from a family who would normally be in grief mode but had nevertheless taken the time to thank her.

She just gave Shelley a friendly wink, at which Shelley laughed for her role in the family prank. Quietly, Lauren knew the whole thing was against all protocols.

She decided to call by her patients in the hostel quarters, ResiCare, while her spirits were lifted. In reality, she wanted to check on Des Jamieson, with whom she had had so little time with and who was high on the CEO's agenda.

When she arrived, she went to the reception desk and signed in. A protocol that had to be upheld. Libby was there and greeted Lauren with a frown.

"What's up Libby - why are you still here?" asked Lauren.

"Patricia called in sick, so I am still here, waiting for Betty to turn up," said Libby, then added, "Sorry to say, Phil Barclay, you've just missed going to PalCare. Surprised you didn't run into the transfer on your way here".

"His tumour pressing even more on his brain?" guessed Lauren.

"His breathing had changed for the worse, his vitals were even more elevated, so we transferred him."

"Oh well, that's OK. He will soon be in a better place." Lauren believed that. She absolutely had to.

"There's more," added Libby.

"Get on with it then," replied Lauren with a sigh.

All of a sudden the happy tingling of the celebration with the family in PalCare was quickly dissipating.

"Desmond Jamieson. God, he is demanding."

"What do you mean?"

"He has been constantly on the phone in his room and that's fine and that's his business, but asking for strong black coffee and light lattes, twice in a matter of hours, and then his very pushy visitor," said Libby.

Lauren looked at the visitor book and made out the name of Vincent Cinelli. She wondered instantly if the name was made up, feeling rather doubtful. He had arrived, according to the register, at 11am and didn't depart until 1.34pm. She almost smirked at the preciseness of the exiting time entry.

Must be a lawyer, was her cynical thought. *Charge them by the minute.*

"He was here for more than two and a half hours, Libby. Any idea of the nature of the visit?" asked Lauren.

"None," said Libby with a huff, adding, "Door was closed."

"OK, thanks," she replied as she headed down the corridor towards Desmond's room.

As she was about to enter, she gave herself a mental check. *Remember Lauren, baby steps, you're still in ice breaking mode.*

When she walked in, she was a little taken aback by the sight of an empty bed. Then to her left, she heard the flushing of a toilet from the ensuite and then the running of water in the basin.

Out came, Des, in cotton pyjamas with the drip trolley at his side, wheeling it towards the bed. He glanced momentarily at Lauren and kept walking towards the bed which was lowered. He had full operation of the remote control – that was obvious to Lauren.

Lauren thought that the patient had certainly gotten his way. He had been unplugged, was now fully dependent and in his own pyjamas.

"How are you going Desmond?" asked Lauren, as the patient sat on the bed.

"Getting there, just not sure where *there* is, Lauren," he replied, and Lauren was happy to hear he had dropped the formalities of *Ms Black.*

"You know, you are rushing the independence thing; there are nursing staff that can help you." Lauren pointed out mildly.

"No need to waste time of the staff, while I can do things on my own."

"And what about the pain?" Lauren asked quickly, not wanting to battle over trivial points.

"Not bad," he said but grimaced as he positioned himself back on the bed and pushed the remote control, first to elevate the bed and then to raise the back portion of the bed to an almost sitting position.

"I see you had a visitor," said Lauren.

"Yes."

"Anything you need to share?"

"No."

"OK," said Lauren, not pushing, then adding, "Did you remember what I said about considering people you may want to contact or be in contact with you."

"Yes."

Monosyllabic responses she had experienced many times before, but they never gave either the questioner or the respondent any satisfaction.

But it was as if Desmond was reading her mind when he then said, "It's not easy imparting information to a stranger, Lauren."

At last, thought Lauren, *engine, ignition, contact and let's see if we have lift-off.*

"I'm not trying to pry into your personal life. I'm just trying to..."

"Help me with preparation and closure?" said Desmond.

"Yes, that's it."

"It's a reality that most of the closure happens after the death."

"What do you mean?"

"You do a lot of your work helping the families of the deceased, isn't that right?"

He didn't wait for a response, adding, "And more with the preparation for the outgoing. Sure, there is closure both sides but, it's like when you go to the funeral, it is more about consoling the living or celebrating with them."

"I guess that's one way of looking at it," Lauren said, a little amazed by the thought that her patient had put into this.

"OK, so let's say we semi-agree with the principles of preparation and closure?" Desmond posed the question.

"What do you mean?"

"I have thought about it and I do want closure," he said.

"Good. So?" posed Lauren.

"I thought about a few people that I need to communicate *closure* with. I just don't know how to go about it," he said, with a glint in his eye that Lauren took as a sign of either regret or fear. She couldn't make out which.

"I'm here to help you Desmond, but that means you have to help me. You have to let me in."

"That's where my problem starts. I've built a business empire based on not trusting people, particularly people I don't know well, and even more so, not letting strangers in at all."

He paused momentarily and then continued, "Or conversely, by employing and in fact, using people that I have deemed to be totally trustworthy. Even then, I am guarded."

"I guess that must be a limiting factor in your life," she replied evenly.

"Perhaps, but other than those closest to me, it has kept me alive," said Desmond.

"So how do we progress, Desmond?"

"Well I know it's Saturday and technically you're not rostered on so let's pick this up on Monday but for me to walk down those unlit tunnels, I need to know who it is I am confiding in."

Lauren felt as if she had just been told by her boss, *You're dismissed now so report to me next week.*

But Lauren also knew, this new patient could head for PalCare before she had the chance to give solace. Too many times on her watch she had seen it happen.

Again Desmond must have been reading her mind when he said, *"Quid pro quo."*

"Are you kidding?" Lauren asked, not loudly but alarmingly.

"Look Desmond, I have done some research, not enough to think I know you, what makes you tick, or even your thoughts on *closure* or *preparation* but one thing I do know, my name is not Clarice, you are not Anthony Hopkins and this is not *Silence of the Lambs,"* she said firmly.

"You are eloquent to say the least, Lauren, and it may be my problem to get over but if you want to help me with closure, which I have said I don't know where to start, I need to have some faith. And I am not referring to a novel or a movie. I am making the statement as it was always meant to be. Think about it, please," Desmond said in a quiet and calm manner.

While her adrenalin was pumping, his very calm, almost disconnected voice had her speechless.

"OK, let's talk on Monday. The staff know to call me if you need anything urgently," she said after counting to ten in her head.

"Thank you," he replied.

"Quid pro quo, even if I think about it, cuts both ways, right?"

"Yes, it does. This for that."

"Who was your visitor last night?" she said, a lump in throat, thinking not to push too hard for fear of losing him altogether.

"He's my lawyer."

She smiled and walked out of the ward. *Charge by the minute.*

***

Chapter Twenty-six

Desmond Jamieson had followed Will Chen's instructions, departing the bloodied hotel room and flown to the Bahamas. He was still dazed by the previous night's experience as he boarded the plane.

He scanned the online media on his laptop, searching for a crime and the real possibility that his client was in a holding cell, waiting to be sentenced.

There was nothing. In fact, in one Singaporean tabloid, there was a picture of Will Chen and a younger woman, smiles beaming from their faces. It was Will's sister accepting a donation at a reception for her chosen charity to research heart disease.

Ironic. Her husband certainly died of heart disease. Lead poisoning to be precise.

Des closed down his laptop and closed his eyes. He was suddenly very tired. His mind wandered to his beautiful Kes who he had left behind almost two years ago. He slept.

***

After the first week at the Ocean Club resort, sipping tropical cocktails and ice cold beers, Des started to consider his next steps. He had a career to forge.

The 1.4 million dollars, which included his consultancy work that had been deposited into his bank account as promised by Will Chen gave him some peace of mind.

Nothing, however, would block out what happened on the 54th floor.

Whichever way he looked at the ordeal, he was incriminated. It was beyond putting up his hand and saying to a magistrate, *"I wasn't there!"* or *"I didn't know that Will Chen was going to shoot a member of his family."*

Reality check, there was no murder, no body, nothing reported.

Will Chen had gotten away with murder and Des wondered if it wasn't the first time.

Amidst his thoughts of the past and the impending future, he made a clear choice to return to Australia and use his network to build a clientele base that required his services.

He placed money on the counter and semi-swivelled in the bar stool he was sitting on. Clumsy, or that is what he confessed to being, as he bumped a young lady with a drink in her hand walking past the bar.

The drink, some concoction that resembled lemon juice with a green tinge, splashed all over the silk dress of the young lady, who did not look impressed at all. More indignant than unimpressed was Des' summation.

The woman, some eight inches shorter than Desmond, just looked up in a semi-shocked, semi-stunned and fully-cross fashion.

"I am so sorry. All my fault. So clumsy of me. I will pay for dry cleaning and everything," stammered Des, his face reddening as he spoke.

A young woman. Slender body, thin nose, pointed chin, long black hair. Those were the characteristics that struck Des in the first instance.

But as they say in the classics, the eyes have it. Hers were a pale shade of hazel that shone. They shone along with the warmth of a radiating smile.

"Don't worry about the dry cleaning," she said, breaking the ice and his initial mesmerisation.

"I insist," said Des, regaining some semblance of thought.

"Shit happens. Why don't you just replace this margarita and we'll call it quits."

"Done deal," said Des, noticing her Asian accent for the first time.

"You're Australian?"

"Ashamedly so and this is not the way we Aussies make introductions. My name is Desmond."

"Hello, Desmond. My name is Janice. Janice Lee."

The fact that her surname was the same as his dead sister's first name, brushed quickly through his thought process, but he was too captivated to dwell on the matter.

***

Desmond Jamieson was quick to fall under the spell of Janice Lee. She was a businesswoman, representing a Malaysian based powerhouse operating out of South East Asia.

A one-week affair dominated with fine dining, passion and sex, underpinned with enjoyment and laughter, so much laughter, saw a change in Desmond he hadn't thought possible.

They promised to keep in touch and indeed they did.

Desmond returned to Australia, realising his reputation had actually grown with his experience in the South East Asian market. While quickly snapped up in employment by one of the 'big four', he had new ventures in mind.

He went out on his own, offering international relationship and business advice including his mainstream accounting and audit services, but extending to trade negotiations.

His business grew like wildfire. He found himself stretched, giving senior counsel to firms, banks and major shareholders. He employed a small team of accountants and auditors but more importantly, an executive assistant named Shirley.

He told Shirley when offering her the position that her main job was to 'keep him honest' which translated to keeping him abreast of all things important, discarding what was not and making sure his schedule remained ruthlessly efficient.

Thankfully, Shirley was extremely good at her job and needed to be, as Des globe-trotted extensively to meet the needs of international and Australian clients.

While his Company was Australian based, he found himself operating more within the South East Asian business community. This, of course, also proved to be very convenient with providing opportunities to be with Janice. Sometimes, this would lead to several weeks together.

Two years into their relationship, he got a phone call from a very tearful Janice Lee.

"What's wrong, Jan?" asked Desmond, instantly picking up on her emotion.

"Des, I am so sorry," she sobbed.

"What? What's happened?"

"I'm pregnant, you're going to be a father. That is, if you want to be..?"

Desmond took a deep breath in, not instantly replying. He steadied himself as unfamiliar emotions rushed through him.

"Des, are you still there?"

"Of course, I am. I'm going to be a father, and nothing could be more wonderful. You're going to be a mother too, of course; is that OK with you?"

"Yes, it is."

"Then, next week, would you mind becoming my wife?"

"Are you serious?"

"Never been more serious in my life."

A week later, Huang Xiaou, aka Will Chen, hosted their lavish wedding reception at none other venue than the 54th floor of crime. Des had initially balked at the idea but realised the generosity behind Will's offer. There were times when Des closed his eyes but the excitement of the extravagant party took over.

Des and Janice Lee-Jamieson remained in Singapore. Des had plenty of work including some new business negotiation projects for Chen. No such thing as a free lunch.

Having said that, Chen regularly deposited one million

U.S. dollars into Will's account every year since that fatal night. Des considered it as hush money at first but in reality Chen was to become one of Des' largest clients for years to come.

Sadly, five months later, Janice went into premature labour with a number of complications. Des was there throughout the entire terrible ordeal, where first he was told the baby was lost, then, while still holding her hand, Janice was also lost to this world.

Des was a shattered man, selfishly considering fate as cruel with two loves of his life gone forever, not including the daughter he never got to know.

It was Chen who again came to the rescue, urging Des to get on with his life.

"Remember when we first met, Desmond?" asked Chen one day, some weeks later.

"I'll never forget," responded Des, somewhat gloomily.

"I knew you were an honest man because you confessed that there was something personal that was holding you back from knowing what you really wanted in life."

Chen didn't wait for a response.

"I always figured that it was a woman from your past and one that you loved dearly, just as you have loved Janice. There will be other women in your life, Desmond, because that is who you are. You are not a loner. You are the type of person who needs company but more importantly, you need someone to care about."

Chen asked for Des to return to Australia to oversee property development negotiations for him on the Gold Coast. Whilst not himself at that point of time, Des realised he had to get back on the horse. Janice Lee would also not want to see him wallow in grief.

Back on a plane travelling home, he pondered over Chen's words, brushing them aside with a level of disbelief usually reserved for flying pigs.

At that moment, he was not to know how insightful Chen was. There would, in fact, be many other women in his life.

Some would give passing pleasure, others endearment and one or two, sheer misery.

Chapter Twenty-seven

On his return to Australia, Des was quick to establish new business ventures, while providing consultancy, auditing and negotiation services to Will Chen. He set up an office, initially in Brisbane and then shortly after, another in Melbourne.

He grieved as he thought of Janice Lee but from time to time, he also thought of Kes and contemplated finding her. He always reconsidered, however, as there was no guarantee of a happy reunion. The years had passed and Kes, no doubt, would be fully ensconced in her own life; a happy one he hoped.

It was when acting on behalf of Will Chen in negotiations for an office building in South Melbourne, that he met Vincent Cinelli. Vincent was a lawyer representing the other party, whom Des found to be softly spoken but articulate. Des was also impressed by his excellent negotiation skills and clear understanding of how to put the necessary contracts in place.

Vincent was thin but one could tell he was very fit, a person that looked after himself, ate well and exercised. He had a long thin, nose and almost hollow cheeks and Des noted his hands with very long fingers and wondered if Vincent played the piano.

After shaking hands at the boardroom table that day, Des invited Vincent to dinner at a nearby restaurant and Vincent amiably accepted.

Des and Vincent traded war stories over dinner; clients they had dealt with and jobs that went well and some that had not.

They shared the normal small talk as well such as where they grew up and football teams they supported. Des had always grown up as a Geelong Cats supporter, while Vincent was clearly one-eyed about the Carlton Blues. Des said that was most unfortunate but they both laughed just the same.

They also shared the love of a good red, a pinot noir or a shiraz. A bottle of each accompanied their expensive dinner that night.

Des spoke of his business structure and his plans to expand which Vincent showed great interest in. Des shared his political views, expressing little trust in any of the major parties which seemed to garner agreement from Vincent with a nod of his head. Finally, Des conveyed his philanthropic interests, saying good business was also a matter of putting back into the community.

"Well," said Desmond as he neatly folded his linen napkin and placed it on the table, "This has been a very pleasant encounter, Vincent, so I thank you."

"Likewise, Desmond," Vincent cordially replied.

"I may have some work for you from time to time, if you are interested?"

"I would look forward to that, Desmond. Let's keep in touch."

That was to be the first of many meetings, many meals and as for *some work for you from time to time,* well, that was the greatest understatement ever to be spoken between them. Vincent was to become Des' lawyer, adviser, confidante, friend and very competitive chess opponent for many years.

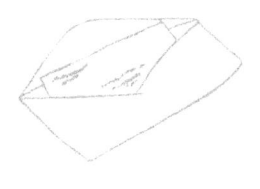

Part Five

The Letters

"Letters are among the most significant memorial a person can leave behind them."

Johann Wolfgang von Goethe

Chapter Twenty-eight

Lauren couldn't get the conversation with Desmond Jamieson out of her head all the way home. In fact, it was to remain lodged deep in her thoughts the remainder of the weekend.

Deliberately trying to avoid her thought process, she asked Alison and her son, Tim, around for a Saturday home-made pizza night. 'Home-made' in the sense of supermarket bases and throwing some creative looking, messy ingredients on the top, sliding the pizza stone into the oven and hoping for the best.

The kids watched Disney re-runs on TV while the adults indulged in too many wines and senseless conversation. Sunday came around all too hastily. Tim had top and tailed in Eileen's double bed while Alison had crashed on the sofa, departing bleary-eyed by 10am the following morning.

Regardless of a night of too much alcohol again, Lauren was wide awake when her overnight guests left, waving them out the door. Wide awake, fully alert, with Desmond Jamieson's words still beckoning her.

It was 11am when her mobile phone rang, and she instantly recognised the ring tone that Eileen had programmed into Lauren's phone as her mother's call sign.

"Hi Mum," answered Lauren.

"Lauren, I just called to see if you are OK?" asked her mother.

"Of course, I am Mum, why wouldn't I be?"

"I don't know, just a dream and that niggling feeling but now I hear your voice, I know I am just being foolish."

"You foolish – never, Mum. The woman who adopted feng shui in every room of her house and then tried to convert it to my much smaller abode? Foolish, never."

"OK, that was a bit overboard," replied Caitlin wryly, knowing that her daughter was taking the mickey out of her.

"It's OK mum, we all have those moments."

"You and Eileen up for a Sunday roast?"

"That sounds really good, chicken I presume?"

"I think I have just taken your dinner order," her mother cheerfully replied.

"We can be there by six, but I have to call into work for a short while this afternoon."

"What about Eileen?"

"She can be patient and come with me; it won't take much more than twenty minutes, if that. See you later," said Lauren, hanging up the phone.

She was determined to set some ground rules on the *quid pro quo* her client had put to her.

Eileen came out of her bedroom, still with sleepy eyes, hearing her mother on the phone.

"Are we going to Gran's?" she asked.

"Yes, roast chicken dinner with all the veg," her mother replied.

"OK, I'll go and shower."

"I have to go to work for a short while on the way. Do you mind?"

"Whatever."

Two hours later, after Lauren had cleaned up from the pizza and wine party from the night before, mother and daughter were in the car heading for City General.

On arrival, she found Belinda Williamson at reception. Belinda aka Bell, aka The Cube. Belinda was five foot nothing and had to practically climb the stool to see over the reception desk she was dutifully guarding.

"Hi Lauren, you're not supposed to be here today, are you?" chirped Belinda, lifting her head from the paperwork she was entering into the computer.

"No, Bell, but just popped in to see Mr Jamieson for a few minutes," said Lauren with a smile, as she dutifully signed the register.

"And how are you going Eileen?" asked Belinda.

"Very well, thank you," replied Eileen, happy for her presence to be acknowledged.

"Let's go, Eileen," said Lauren as she started to quickly walk down the corridor towards Des Jamieson's room.

The door was open but yet again, Des was not in his bed. The door to the small garden area outside was also open.

"Just stay here Eileen, I won't be long, I promise," beckoned Lauren, leaving her daughter in the corridor, as she crossed the room to go to the garden.

Des was sitting outside at the small glass table with a notebook and pen. Sensing Lauren's presence, he closed the notebook and looked up, signalling Lauren to take the seat opposite.

"Not here for long, Des. I'm on the way to see my mother and just thought I would drop in to see how you are faring," said Lauren, as she sat down.

Des smiled.

"That's very good of you Lauren; I wasn't expecting to see you until after the weekend. Just thought I would sit outside for a while. Get some fresh air and all that."

Lauren sensed something different in her patient but couldn't quite put her finger on exactly what it was. There was a gleam in his eye, and he seemed calm. Serene.

Des glanced towards his room, noticed someone standing outside, silhouetted in the corridor, then turned his head back to Lauren.

"You have been thinking about our last conversation," he said in a matter of fact way. It was not a question. It was a statement.

"Yes, I have," said Lauren.

"Well?"

"It doesn't fit comfortably with me. It's not my normal modus operandi."

"I see."

"Let me finish. I am a very private person and I think you are, too. Sure, you are the big businessman and you're well known but I don't think there are too many people that *really* know you. Does that sound right?"

"Perceptive enough."

"I don't want you to delve too deeply into my personal life, either, so baby steps and we'll see how it goes."

"Quid pro quo."

"Quid pro quo," repeated Lauren with almost a sense of resignation but she knew she would lose him to silence otherwise.

Des glanced again towards the silhouetted figure across the room and then back to Lauren.

"My daughter, Eileen," said Lauren before the question could be asked.

"And her father?"

"We're not going there now. Have you thought of the people you would like to contact?" asked Lauren, taking back the upper hand.

"Yes," he said, hesitating, but then, opening the notebook, he tore out a page, folded it and handed it to Lauren.

"Thank you, Des," she said, knowing how hard it must be for the man who, as he had stated, had trusted very few in his lifetime.

She rose to leave and said thank you again.

"Perhaps, I can meet Eileen one day," said Des.

"Perhaps," replied Lauren, turning and heading back to her daughter.

Quid pro quo thought Des, as he watched her leave. Communicating with the people on the list he had just handed Lauren filled him with apprehension.

Chapter Twenty-nine

Returning to the car, Lauren unfolded the piece of paper. There were only a few names on the list. A couple of names, she recognised from her initial computer searches.

She smiled, thinking she had indeed had a breakthrough. Jamieson was open to communicating to others before his final demise. Based on her first conversation with her patient, she had almost considered this an impossibility.

Then, as she drove, with Eileen now with headphones plugged into her ears, listening to whatever music she chose, Lauren thought of Amelia Schwartz's warning. *He will be manipulative.*

Had she just been played? Her smile turned to a frown very quickly but then, she convinced herself that was not the case. After all, she had swiftly closed down that question about her ex-husband, never promised him that he would meet her daughter.

She thought about that for a moment and wondered if the *'Perhaps, I can meet Eileen one day?'* was yet another mind game. Was he really the manipulative person that her CEO described?

What the hell? Why would I introduce my daughter to a man who is dying? Fuck that for an idea. Fuck Des Jamieson and his quid pro quo. Some things were sacrosanct. I am the case specialist, I know what's right.

Her temperature dropped a little and just as well, as she closed hard on the brakes before the traffic lights ahead.

Amber. Red. Stop.

Beside her, Eileen removed her ear plugs and looked at her mother, alarm in her young eyes.

"Mum, what the....?"

It's OK, we're OK," Lauren replied, reaching for the bottle of water in the console, taking a large gulp.

The lights turned green and Lauren accelerated, pretending her temporary lack of concentration had passed. *Concentrate, geez Lauren, pull yourself together,* she thought, shaking her head to try and clear her thoughts.

"Are you alright mum?" Eileen asked kindly.

"I'm fine Eils, just need to focus. We'll have a nice dinner at Gran's and then home to bed for me."

Eileen remained quiet, not convinced. Lauren, in an attempt to change the subject, asked her daughter what she was listening to on the headphones plugged into her mobile phone.

Please, don't say punk rock or heavy metal. Neither of the genres met Lauren's comprehension.

"Listening to a lot of stuff, Mum," her daughter replied.

"Such as..?"

"I just listened to *'What we did for love'.*"

"What band sings that?"

"No band, it's one of Gran's favourites. I think it's Johnny Mathis. Have you heard the song?"

"Only one million times, Eils, one million times," said Lauren smiling.

Eileen went quiet wondering what *one million times* actually meant. Lauren broke the silence again.

"Can't you Bluetooth that to the radio player in the car?" she quizzed Eileen.

"Sure, just give me a minute," Eileen said, beaming.

Moments later, the technological wizard that Eileen was in her mother's eyes had the masterful velvet vibrato voice of Johnny Mathis playing through the car speakers.

"Kiss the day goodbye..."

Chapter Thirty

It was eight o'clock in the evening, after enjoying a delicious Sunday roast at her mother's house, when Lauren and Eileen arrived home.

"Eileen, half an hour then bed, it's a school night," Lauren directed.

Her daughter raised her eyes to the ceiling and shrugged her shoulders, then walked into the family room and switched on the television.

There was a knock on the front door. Seriously, not tonight, Alison – was her first thought as she opened the door.

But to her dismay, there was no Alison. Instead Jack Bissen stood there before her. She hardly recognised her ex-husband, with his eyes darting side-to-side like a neon light on its last charge.

"Well, aren't you going to ask me in?" he said with what may have been a smirk, but with one look into his eyes, Lauren could tell he was half stoned; on what, she couldn't be sure.

"You know you are not allowed here," said Lauren defiantly.

His rank, alcohol-laden breath hot in her face, Bissen pushed Lauren aside and walked into the entry hallway.

"Get the fuck out of here," screamed Lauren.

Lauren stepped around him, facing him and standing her ground, certain he would go no further.

"Relax babe," he drooled, "I just wanted to check in and see how you were doing."

"We're doing fine, so get out." Lauren retorted.

"Yeah, well, I'm doing it tough; could do with some cash. What about it, babe?"

"No way, not this time Jack, not now, not ever again."

Their voices were escalated enough to arouse Eileen whose eyes had been transfixed by the Disney channel. She entered the hallway just in time to see her father slap her mother hard across the face. Lauren hit the wall and then crumpled to the floor.

"Leave mum alone, you bastard," shrieked Eileen.

"It's OK, little darling," slurred the groggy Bissen, "Mummy and I just not seeing eye to eye."

Distracted by Eileen, Bissen didn't notice that Lauren, having hit the floor in shock, was now standing, brandishing a baseball bat that she kept in the corner next to the front door. First, she pointed the club at his face and then swung hard into his midriff and knocked the wind out of him.

He was totally stunned, gasping for breath.

"Get the fuck out of my house and don't you ever try to come back," Lauren growled.

Bissen wheezed all the way to the front door and staggered out. This was not the result he had in mind.

Mother and daughter embraced; their tears rolled down, blending on their cheeks.

"It's OK, Eils, he's just not a well person," said Lauren.

"That's not right mum; he's evil."

Lauren did not respond. She walked to the kitchen, opened the freezer door and slapped a pack of frozen peas on her left cheekbone, which was now throbbing from the ordeal.

She double-checked every lock on the doors and windows, then walked Eileen to her bedroom and lay down next to her daughter until Eileen was asleep. Trying to stay awake with frozen peas on her face, hugging her daughter, Lauren eventually succumbed to the fatigue of the day.

***

Monday morning came around swiftly. Lauren had woken in the middle of the night, dispensed with the damp, soggy bag of peas and slept in her own bed.

On awakening, she did her ablutions. Toilet, shower and then, horror as she looked into the mirror for the first time. Regardless of the peas, a nasty bruise was forming on her left cheek.

She was never a big make-up person; perhaps some light rouge on the cheeks, some moisturiser on her skin and that was it. Today, she wanted to hide past scars or at the very least, fresh bruising.

She told herself to get a grip and, as mothers do, got her daughter up, breakfasted and ready for school. Thankfully, Eileen was of an age where she didn't need to be driven to school. Instead, Eileen and Tim usually walked the five blocks together.

Just the same, Lauren was still behind schedule and needed to hustle to get to work as planned. Eileen did not mention the intrusion of the night before and didn't question the makeup. She gave her mother a tight hug before dashing out the door to meet Tim.

As it turned out Lauren arrived at work at her normal time with a few minutes to spare. On arrival at ResiCare reception the ever-reliable Libby was on duty as Lauren signed the register, duly noting the time.

"What's up Libby; you seem to be doubling shifts?" quizzed Lauren.

"Well Lauren, I take it when I can. Three kids finishing primary school and the twins about to go to high school, who couldn't do with the extra cash?" She shrugged and smiled.

"Just don't overdo it Libby, keep some of the energy to enjoy the time with the kids."

"Look who's talking; I see three calls to you over the weekend." Libby made a face.

"Goes with the territory Libby," Lauren responded with a sigh.

"Well, sorry to break the news Lauren, but upstairs admin dropped down a new file with your name on it."

"I could have guessed that was going to be the case, Libby. A couple have dropped off after all – hospitals are all about quotas. Hand it over."

Libby handed over an inch thick file, full of medical notes, patient background, personal material, current status and prognosis; indicating potential longevity.

It was a woman, just 38 years of age with ovarian cancer. Her name: Caroline Withers. Her initial glance at the file informed Lauren that the patient had opted for ResiCare, knowing PalCare was to quickly follow.

The patient was a realist and brave in her reality. *Just not fair*, thought Lauren.

Having read the morning report on her other patients, she was comfortable enough to tuck the Withers file under her arm as she headed towards the room holding her *quid pro quo* nemesis.

She walked staunchly down one corridor and the next, Amelia Schwartz's warning ringing in her ears of how this patient would manipulate her. She had taken the hand-folded piece of paper that Desmond had given her from her skirt pocket, studied it one more time and readied herself for the challenge.

Quid pro quo, indeed. She just needed to do her job.

When Lauren walked into Des' room that morning, he was sitting in one of the two armchairs that sat each side of a small round table. He could not help but note that something was different about her. She seemed a little strained and for someone who always dressed impeccably, a little more make-up than usual.

The other thing that he took notice of was her fragrance. Her perfume was delightful and while he could not put his finger on it, he hadn't noticed her wearing the same scent in previous meetings.

Lauren sat down in the opposite armchair, placing a black compendium on the table, which held a writing pad and pen and also the folded note that Des had given her listing the names of people he potentially wanted to reach out to, during whatever time he had left.

"How are you feeling, Des?" asked Lauren.

"Not too bad," he replied, pointing at the drip stand. "I pump a little more juice in from time to time."

"Good, there is no need to be in pain if it can be helped."

She could not help but notice his steady gaze towards her. She felt self-conscious and wondered whether the makeup was hiding the bruise on her cheek adequately.

"I have looked at your list, Des and I am a little puzzled," she pushed on.

"Puzzled?"

"I can understand your son Ryan but your first wife, Janice Lee, she passed away a long time ago, didn't she?"

"Yes, and I was there when she passed, but you see Lauren, I never got the chance to tell her how much I cared and how much I loved her, before she died."

"I see," said Lauren, "So what do you want to do?"

"I want to write a letter. It won't be a long letter, but I want to say what I should have said a long time ago."

"So, this is a letter that technically will never be posted."

"That's right. You think it foolish, don't you?'

"No, Des, I don't. You have been holding this in your subconscious for a long time so I think it will be good for you to have that closure. If you tell me what you want to say, I can write it down and type it up for you."

"Probably best. I think my handwriting is somewhat scratchy at the moment."

"OK, so let's start."

Des cleared his throat and for a moment closed his eyes as if he was preparing to deliver a political speech.

Opening his eyes, he started to dictate a letter to his dead wife.

"My dearest, Janice Lee. You were not the first woman that I loved; nor were you the last, but I loved you with all my heart just the same.

"I know we should have spent more time together in our early days, but you had your career and I had mine. To think we met over the spilling of a margarita - that was one of the luckiest moments of my life.

"When you rang me so tearful and so fearful that you were pregnant and didn't know how I would take the news, I was filled with joy, I cannot to this day ever understand. I was so happy with the thought of becoming a father and got on the very next plane to be beside you.

"Will Chen hosted our wedding and it was such a blissful time. My deepest sadness came when we first lost baby Mia, and then I lost you to this world.

"You were so brave, my darling and I would have done anything to have saved you. All my love, your husband and lover, Desmond Jamieson."

Lauren put the pen down and looked across the table. Her patient's eyes glistened with tears which with one hand, he silently wiped away.

"That was beautiful, Des, truly beautiful," she said softly, a lump in her throat and a small tear in her eye as well.

"You were right Lauren; I should have spoken a long time ago. I was too distraught, too selfish, that I couldn't even bring myself to talk at her funeral."

"Sometimes grief makes it very hard to speak. Do you want to go on to the next one on your list?"

"No, that's enough for the moment, but I would appreciate you typing it up for me please."

"OK," said Lauren, starting to stand up.

"Where are you going?"

"I'm going to type this up and do my rounds."

"Not before quid pro quo, Lauren."

"Ah. What do you want to know?"

"How you came to have that bruise on your left cheek."

"Would you believe I was clumsy enough to run into a door?"

"No."

Lauren practically fell back into the chair, took a deep sigh and while she thought it unwise, for reasons unknown to her, she nevertheless began her story.

***

"My ex-husband," she slightly stammered, not knowing which way to look but eventually raising her head to eye her patient directly.

After all, he just shared a very raw, personal part of his life with me and I know this is not protocol and I don't know why, but here goes.

"This is Eileen's father you are talking about?" asked Des.

"Yes, he came around last night, regardless of restraining orders, looking for money and he slapped me hard."

"I'm sorry." Desmond's mouth compressed in a thin line.

"It's OK, I can tell you he will have a very sore midriff and ribs today. I swing a pretty mean baseball bat."

She gave a wry smile and Des returned it with his own, along with a nod of the head of approval.

"Does this happen often? Did you call the police?"

"No. And no. It wasn't always like this," she said.

Des waited for her to continue and after a moment or two, she went on.

"I was on placement at a hospital in Windsor in my last year of university, when I met Jack, Jack Bissen, at a bar after work. He was a high-powered, highly energised salesman, charismatic to say the least. He took me to dinners and shows and I was taken by his charm.

"We married and I fell pregnant with Eileen and that's when the wheels started to fall off. He was often away on the road doing his job, or at least that's what I thought. The pressure of the job, I think, took its toll, or at least that's the excuse I allowed him. I discovered he was taking recreational drugs. I tried to get him help but then I discovered our bank balance was shrinking.

"He was cheating on me as well. I didn't know but one day I picked up his mobile phone when it rang and a woman's voice started talking dirty about how much she had enjoyed the other night, not realising I was on the line.

"He started getting into hard drugs and I had no choice but to kick him out. I wanted to restart my career which I had put on hold when I had Eileen. And most of all, I was a sole parent wanting to protect her daughter.

"He tried to see me at the hospital, again at Windsor. That was the job I had before coming here. He was trying to make up and begged for someone to help him. I had a small cabinet in the shared office which housed drugs such as pethidine and other painkillers. I went to find a clinician or one of the drug counsellors.

"I stupidly had left the keys to the cabinet on my desk. When I returned, the cabinet was open and he was gone. It almost cost me my job but the police followed him up. He was stoned, well and truly, mixing any and every drug he could find.

"He's been gone ever since until last night and he looks nothing like the man I met all those years ago. I divorced him ages ago and reverted back to my maiden name."

Tears sprang in Lauren's eyes. She quickly reached for the Kleenex box next to Des' bed, brushing them away and blowing her nose.

"Thank you for telling me Lauren. I want to make sure he doesn't worry you again," said Des.

"Ha, I never thought I would open up like that. And you can't protect me. That's why I have the baseball bat. Anyway, I must go, letter to type and rounds to make," said Lauren and with that she took a deep breath, bundled up the compendium and left the room.

Chapter Thirty-one

Vincent Cinelli was sitting in his office going over paperwork that would close two of Desmond's investment portfolios when his mobile rang. It was Desmond himself, and Vincent thought that his timing was just plain uncanny.

"Hi Des," greeted Vincent.

"Vincent, there's something I want you to look into for me," said Desmond.

Twenty minutes later, the phone call complete, Vincent was the one making a call, this time to the Assistant Commissioner of Police, Alfred McDougall. After a brief delay, McDougall's personal assistant switched Vincent through.

"McDougall here," the familiar gruffness echoed through the phone.

Vincent could picture him, having met the man on a few occasions with Desmond. A couple of times when Desmond had sponsored the Police Commissioner's annual ball and once or twice when Alfred McDougall had returned the favour at hospital fundraisers.

McDougall was a giant of a man, standing six-foot-six and rock-hard solid with a slightly bent nose and dark bushy eyebrows that seemed to make his towering presence even more formidable.

"Vincent Cinelli here, Alfred," replied Vincent.

"Ah, Vincent, how are things? How is Des?"

"Not good, I'm afraid. It's a matter of time, perhaps a few weeks or less. I really don't know."

"I'm really sorry to hear that, Vince."

"I'm calling for a bit of a favour, please, Alfred. Something for Desmond."

"I'm listening."

"He has a carer by the name of Lauren Black and Lauren has evidently been roughed up by her ex, some kind of low-life druggie."

"His name, it's also Black..?"

"No, his name is Jack Bissen."

"You're kidding? Huh."

"Why would I be kidding?"

"Just by coincidence, a file on your low-life came my way this morning."

"Well, that is a coincidence."

"He is indeed a low-life, but a really dumb one at that. He robbed a couple of teens in Fitzroy. These kids went to the local station and reported it with a very clear description. Nothing has come from it. But guess who one of the kids is?"

"Go, on."

"The boy is the son of Justin Kale."

"The Emergency Services minister?"

"Yep, one and the same."

"Dumb is right."

"Well I got a call from Kale complaining of the inaction, so I now have an internal affairs headache."

"Sorry to hear that Alfred, it sounds like a royal pain in the arse, but Desmond wants his carer protected from any further issues with her ex."

"Don't tell anyone what I've just told you, especially the carer, and leave this with me. I aim to get on top of it within a couple of days. I have your number; I'll give you a call."

"Thanks, Alfred," said Vincent and he hung up the phone.

McDougall had a bad feeling about the whole affair. Based on the file, the Senior Constable at the Fitzroy station, Michael

Fagan, had written up the report himself. It was dated and signed by the two victims of Jack Bissen.

The name of the witness did not even ring a warning bell for Fagan; that the boy was related to the Emergency Services minister. Disturbingly and according to the law enforcement assistance program, aka the LEAP system, there had been no further action.

In McDougall's mind, the whole thing reeked. It was either one of total incompetence at best or corruption at worst. Neither prospect pleased him, but the latter was nothing less than abhorrent.

Of course, considering his status in the force, if he were to show up personally to investigate, all would go to ground, records manipulated, and corruption swiftly covered up, if in fact, corruption existed.

He picked up the phone and hit the speed dial for one Detective Sean Alderman. Alderman was an excellent detective who knew how to get a job done, especially in investigating internal issues such as this. McDougall considered Sean Alderman to be one of his most reliable officers.

Alderman picked up the phone instantly on recognising the caller was Assistant Commissioner McDougall. McDougall asked if Alderman was available for a coffee, which invoked an affirmative response. They agreed to meet at 2pm at Krystal's café, an old fashioned 60s-style café with booths where they could talk in private.

Chapter Thirty-two

Lauren, having done the rounds of her patients, was sitting in her office doing paperwork; mandatory client reports informing of current status, issues and anything else that was relevant to movement from ResiCare to PalCare. However, she was having difficulty focusing on the task at hand. She couldn't get Des Jamieson out of her head or the fact that she had revealed so much about her life to him.

Had she played into his hands too easily with the whole *quid pro quo* thing? Had she been manipulated as Amelia Schwartz had alluded to as a possibility?

And yet, she felt a sense of relief for having the experience of telling someone about one of the saddest parts of her life. And not just someone; a patient, Des Jamieson. If asked why, she would not be able to give an answer.

Her computer pinged with an incoming email. The subject line: Des Jamieson. The scribe was Amelia Schwartz. *Just plain scary*, thought Lauren. She opened the email which simply read:

> *Hi Lauren,*
> *Can you tell me how Desmond is doing please?*
> *Amelia*

Obviously, Lauren's head was not the only one filled with thoughts of Mr. Jamieson. She quickly typed a response.

> *Hi Amelia,*
> *He is doing as well as expected. He seems to be very*

determined to remain independent – for how long, I can't say but I can advise you he has opened up and is writing letters of closure to people. I'm just about to type up one for him now.

Regards,

Lauren

Lauren opened Word on her computer and started to type Des' letter to Janice Lee. A couple of minutes later, she was on her way back to Des' room with the letter in hand.

To her surprise Des had a visitor sitting precisely where she had sat a few hours earlier. The small table, however, was taken up by a large and ornate chessboard. Des looked up and motioned Lauren to come forward.

"Lauren, this is Vincent Cinelli; Vincent, this is Lauren, whom I have mentioned to you," said Des.

Vincent stood up and shook Lauren's hand with a cordial smile. "Nice to meet you," Lauren said politely.

"I am very grateful for the care you are giving Des, Lauren," Vincent said.

"That's what I am here for," she answered, "I'm sorry to disturb you, but I have that letter for you, Des."

"Thank you Lauren, that was quick," replied Des taking the letter from Lauren.

"As you can see, Vincent and I are in battle over a bit of chess."

"The truth is, Lauren, I think he cheats," said Vincent with a wink of the eye.

The two men chuckled.

"Well, I'll leave you to it," said Lauren, turning to make her escape.

"Thank you again, Lauren. It means a lot to me," said Des, holding the folded letter up.

"Perhaps we can look at your list again tomorrow," she suggested, as she turned again to walk out the door.

On her way back to her office, Lauren couldn't help thinking how strange things were. Her patient, a dying man, playing chess with his lawyer. She imagined the cash register ringing up the fees. They charged in six-minute increments, didn't they?

Chapter Thirty-three

Detective Sean Alderman apologised for being a few minutes late and took the red leather bench seat opposite McDougall, who had positioned himself at the booth at the rear of Krystal's café.

They both ordered cappuccinos, McDougall opting for light milk, Alderman regular, which was not that surprising. Alderman always looked a little podgy and was much shorter than the towering McDougall. He had a shaved head and a five o'clock shadow that seemed to be a permanent fixture on his face.

With the two coffees in front of them, McDougall got straight to the point and relayed the story of the Emergency Services minister's son and his girlfriend. He didn't mention Des Jamieson or his carer.

Alderman listened intently, only interrupting once to ask whether Fagan had been under question any other time in his career. McDougall responded in the negative, but added that the local drug scene had gotten worse in the vicinity with very few charges being laid.

Once McDougall had finished his summation, Alderman rubbed the dark stubble on his chin and looked at his half-empty cup of coffee.

"Think I might do some tagging for a couple of days," he finally said.

"I'll leave that up to you, Sean," said McDougall.

"I'll find Bissen and will keep watch over Fagan. Who knows, their paths may just cross."

"I just need to keep this quiet. We don't need a police corruption story hitting the tabloids right now."

"Understood," said Sean, standing to shake the Assistant Commissioner's hand and then leaving the café and the bill for the senior officer to pay.

***

Before leaving the office which was crammed with half a dozen workstations, mostly stacked with piles of paper and files, and a few coffee mugs crying out for a wash, Sean Alderman checked the LEAP system and printed out a mug shot of one, Jacob aka Jack, Travis Bissen.

He noted that Bissen had been arrested for drug theft from a hospital some years ago but had been let off as a first-time offender. Sean snorted with disgust – *a druggie is a druggie is a druggie. All it meant was he hadn't been caught all the other times.*

Sean headed out to the car park and climbed into his car, a classic 1963 Mini Minor, which his smart suit-wearing colleagues ridiculed him over. Some jibed that they admired the two-tone look; another joke at the car's faded green tinge and rust.

The car, however, was still reliable and it suited him down to a tee. While his brothers-in-arms wore polished black or tan shoes and crisply pressed suits, he went about his detective work by *flying under the radar*. The unshaven and scruffy look suited his modus operandi and his persona just fine. Sean Alderman got results.

He placed the key into the chamber and turned it to the right, followed by a push of the button on the floor of the car, and with a slight splutter and a jerk of the gear stick, he was off and heading to the backstreets of Fitzroy.

Like most inner suburbs, there was the good and the bad. Fitzroy was no different but some of the bad was horrific. Horrific, and at times, dangerous. If someone wanted to score drugs, they wandered into the most seedy areas, where predators lurked.

Sean knew it only too well. He had grown up here but as he turned into one of the *darker* side streets, he reminisced and decided that the neighbourhood had, if anything, deteriorated. *Could that actually be possible?* With this thought in mind, he parked his car, and his spirits were instantly raised.

He couldn't believe his luck. A mere fifty yards up the road, in the shadows of a factory door, was none other than Jack Bissen or at least a grimier version. He pulled out the mug-shot print and while some years had passed and the man he was looking at was, no doubt, worse for wear, he was convinced he had found his target.

Bissen was just standing in the doorway, smoking a cigarette or reefer. Sean couldn't tell which, from his sitting position. He decided to stay in the car and observe for a while longer.

Ten minutes had passed, when a young man in a three-piece suit walked up the street and crossed to where Bissen was standing. Sean reached under the passenger seat and quietly retrieved his auto-SLR camera with telescopic lens.

The young man showed hesitation, looking in all directions while Sean remained undetected. On reaching Bissen, the young man spoke first, and Jack nodded his head.

There were a few more words exchanged. This time Bissen shook his head. Sean had already zoomed in and taken three photos. The young man took out his wallet and put what Sean estimated to be three hundred dollars into Bissen's waiting hand. More shots; the shutter sounding its familiar *phhtt-phtt* noise.

Come on Jack, make the deal. Sean had seen it all before and then, Eureka! Jack Bissen handed over a small bag of white stuff to the other man. *Phhtt-phhtt.*

The young man was quick to walk away, passing Sean's car as he ducked down low in the seat, pretending to look at his map.

Sean had no interest in the man right now. He had the photos if required.

He did, however, have great interest in Bissen who had already started to walk in the opposite direction. Sean got out of the car and crossed the street, starting to tail Bissen from the opposite side of the road.

Sean stepped up his pace and had passed Bissen, allowing the detective to cross the street and intercept his target before reaching the next corner, where an empty warehouse covered with graffiti stood with sunshine glinting off its broken windows.

Bissen, on the other hand, was happy with his slow amble and even happier with the amount he had stung his customer just a few minutes ago.

"Happy, Jack..?"

Sean's question stopped Bissen in his tracks, making him look up for the first time.

"Who the fuck are you?" asked Bissen with distaste.

"I hope to be a happy customer, Jack, just like the young guy that just slung you a few hundred."

"How do you know my name?"

"Everyone knows your name, Jack. You're one of the most reliable suppliers around. So, what about it?"

"So what about it!? I don't know you from a bar of soap, mate, so piss off!"

"Not friendly, Jack. As for a bar of soap, don't think you've seen one in a while."

"Piss off!"

"Here, Jack, I have the money," said Sean, reaching for his wallet.

"This a set-up?" asked Jack, diverted from his suspicions by the wallet in Sean's hand.

"I just want some of the happy stuff, Jack. It's good stuff, isn't it?"

"Course; I don't deal with bad shit," said Jack, greed overcoming caution.

He reached into the pocket of his shabby coat and showed a small plastic bag of white powder.

"How much?"

"That's all I've got on me; you can have it for couple of green ones."

"Great," said Sean, pulling out his mobile phone, "Just need to turn this off."

"Fuck, you a cop?" Jack's expression looked like thunder.

Sean had already pulled out his badge.

"Not just a cop, Jack; I'm a detective."

Sean could tell by the rapid movement of Bissen's beady eyes, that the felon was about to make a dash for it. Sean was quicker than Bissen's panicked impulses, which the reefer had dulled. He grabbed the drug-pusher's coat collar and slammed him into the brick warehouse wall, followed by a sharp jab into his solar plexus.

"Jesus Christ, why does everyone have to hit me in the guts?" Jack wheezed.

"You OK, Jack?" asked Sean, feigning concern.

"This is fucking entrapment," whined Jack.

"It's OK, Jack. I just want to have a talk with you. I'm not taking you in or at least, not if I get what I need."

"Here, you can take the crap," said Jack endeavouring to pick up the drugs that had fallen from his hand in the scuffle.

"No, Jack, I don't want that crap. Who knows what's in it?" Sean kicked the bag away.

"What the fuck do you want?"

"Well Jack, you're in real deep."

"What do ya mean?"

"A few weeks ago, you stole from a couple of kids."

"Don't know what ya talking about," said Jack, but his eyes were darting from side to side with panic.

"The problem is, Jack, you picked the wrong targets," Sean continued, "You picked on the son of a government minister."

"Fuck."

"Yes, fuck indeed."

"What do ya want?" asked Jack, now very resigned to the fact that he was, as the copper had said, *in deep*.

As if Sean could read the scared rabbit's mind, he said, "Yes, Jack, real deep. And do you know why?"

"Why?" spat Jack, wanting to snort the contents of the bag. Anything, to take him away from this nightmare.

"Your mate, Michael Fagan at Fitzroy police station; he's dobbed you in."

"Bullshit! No way, he gets..." Bissen's voice trailed off.

"Gets what, Jack? Doesn't really matter," said Sean.

"He wouldn't do it."

Sean just maintained eye contact and Jack Bissen started to feel a cold trickle of doubt.

"Well Jack, he has, he's thrown you right under the bus, but you can get off this real light."

"What do I have to do?"

Chapter Thirty-four

Lauren returned to work the next day after a restless night's sleep.

For a while, she had found some form of solace, a release of deep anguish by divulging so much about herself to her patient the day before. Then as she had tossed and turned in her bed, the little voice of doubt sprang from nowhere.

Her professionalism could be called into question. On the emotional scale, her job was to take in, not give out. Yet she had found some strange form of comfort in talking to her patient.

The job was tough and she was good at it. She knew when she needed to, she had the employee assistant program to talk to. EAP was only a phone call away and then there were the mandatory six-month counselling sessions which allowed people in her position to talk openly about how they were coping with the many stresses of the job.

She loved her work, although at times, she was weary from its constant demand. She did not want a perceived breach of protocol to threaten her position at the hospital and more so, her position at ResiCare.

Still, she had found talking to Des Jamieson to be calming. She likened it to writing to a pen-pal; she could share her deepest thoughts, but the relationship was still distant enough to step away from if the response was not a happy one.

She turned over in bed again restlessly. Yes, unburdening

herself to Jamieson had been reassuring, and she wondered if it was that calming ability to listen so intently that was the reason he had worked his way up the corporate ladder.

She had finally fallen into a deep sleep at three in the morning but duly responded to the alarm clock at six.

Lauren gathered her thoughts amidst the morning routine, making sure Eileen was up and ready for school. Today was Thursday and she had already asked Alison to take Eileen on to netball practice after school, knowing she had a joint carers meeting late in the afternoon.

She promised she would be home well before Eileen was delivered home from practice and told her friend that pasta would be ready for the evening meal for all four of them.

***

When Lauren arrived that morning, her mind was still conflicted. She picked up her morning report from reception, detailing status of her patients and retreated to her office with little conversation with the staff. She felt out of sorts and skipped her normal small talk with colleagues, reception and nursing staff.

Lauren turned on her computer and sighed as she heard the familiar whirring sound. She sat down and as always, took in her office surroundings, which seemed a little drab in the cold morning light. *Perhaps it's time for a refresh.*

Looking at the morning report, two things stuck out immediately. Phillip Barclay had finally passed away, only a day or two after being transferred to PalCare.

Poor Phil, she thought. He had no idea of who he was, or where, for that matter. *I'd better get the paperwork started for him.* Another sigh.

The other item that was glaring was in relation to Desmond Jamieson. His blood pressure had lowered and they had monitored his heart overnight but then conditions improved. There was a notation to advise that the patient had again requested the freedom to move around, drip in tow.

Stubborn bastard. Always gets what he wants.

Still, while conditions had improved, they were telling signs and for Lauren, she had more work to do with this patient.

Her computer screen had come to life and she logged in. Checking a long list of incoming emails, she spotted one from Amelia Schwartz, in response to her email from the day before.

> *Hi Lauren,*
>
> *That is indeed welcome news. I'm not sure how you got the surly bugger to open up but whatever you are doing, keep it up.*
>
> *Well done.*
>
> *Amelia.*

Suddenly, her doubts and insecurities paled into insignificance. Maybe, just maybe, she had caught the right tram after all

Chapter Thirty-five

Senior Constable of Fitzroy police Michael Fagan strolled into the park, his normal rendezvous point to meet local scumbag, Jack Bissen.

The drug-crazed Bissen had fit the description as the offender responsible for a bag snatch mugging at a local supermarket two days ago. Fagan had again met with the victim at the station front counter and had duly written up a report with a promise to 'Look into it.'

Fagan thought he needed to curb some of Bissen's erratic behaviour, without threatening the booty that the low-life provided.

Fagan scanned the circumference of the small park; the rusted slide, the half-broken swing upon which Bissen was sitting, bleary-eyed as ever. *Off his face, no doubt*, Fagan surmised sourly.

He also noted two homeless people, one lying to his left, motionless on the park bench which was missing planks of wood; the other, unmoving, propped on the ground with his back against the dying plane tree on the opposite side.

Fagan considered he might well be dead and if not, he presumed there would be pointy ends of dirty, used needles protruding from the ground into his arse. Either, way neither of the filthy derelicts would bother him.

He did, however, walk past the one lying on the park bench. He could smell the stench of cheap alcohol within three feet and just make out the face of an unshaven *good-for-nothing*. The top of a shabby green jacket poked above a threadbare blanket riddled with holes. Fagan gave the body a nudge, which seemed to stir slightly. Then Fagan noted the bottle in the brown paper bag and the drool from the man's lips seeping into his unshaven chin.

"Fucking derro," Fagan said dismissively, as he walked onward to the swing that Bissen was sitting on, rocking back and forth.

Fagan thought that Bissen must be off his face on drugs as he remained static as he neared. Normally, Bissen would be standing, nervous and almost twitching.

"So you sent another fucking victim to me, Jack? What the hell," began Fagan.

"Doesn't matter anymore, does it, you fuckwit," responded Bissen listlessly.

"Who do you think you're talking to? What are you talking about?"

"Doesn't matter, let's get this over with. You wanna punch me in the guts, too?"

"No, Jacky boy, I'm in a benevolent mood. How much did you take from the old girl at the supermarket?"

"She only had three hundred; hardly worth it."

"Well let's call it one hundred. As I said, I'm in a benevolent mood, so do you have a bit of smack for me?"

Jack Bissen stood up from the swing, reached into his pocket for a small bag of white stuff and handed it into Fagan's waiting palm. It was at that moment that Fagan caught a glimpse of movement to the far left of him.

"Stop right there, Michael," came the command from the bench seat.

Fagan turned around and saw the so-called derelict was standing, with police revolver in one hand and badge in the other.

"It's OK; I am here to arrest this felon," cried Fagan, quickly recovering from his initial shock.

The second homeless person that had been slumped against the tree was also now standing.

"You are under arrest, Michael Fagan," said the disguised police officer.

"No, no. You've got this all wrong, boys," said Fagan.

"I'm Detective Sean Alderman, and you are under arrest," asserted the man from the bench, who only a few moments ago had been hugging a bottle and appeared to have spittle seeping from his mouth.

"And I am Detective Colin Walker," said the tree man.

Fagan was rattled, and whirled back towards Jack Bissen, who was stealthily beginning to edge away.

"Stop Jack, you're under arrest too," said Sean, trying to regain control of the spiralling situation.

"What, you said.." Jack protested.

Overcome with rage at the doublecross, Fagan yanked his revolver from its holster and shot Bissen in the chest. He dropped to the ground with a dull thump. Sean quickly lowered his sights and shot Fagan in the leg just below his kneecap. Fagan fell to the ground in agony and Walker moved swiftly to kick the gun from his hand, roll him over and cuff him regardless of the injury.

Sean was already calling it in as their backup was only one block away as planned.

"Get the paramedics here. Pronto!" barked Sean. "We've got two down."

He walked up to Jack Bissen and realised any ambulance was going to be too late for him. Not the exact result that the detective had hoped for, but the job was done, and his plan had been well executed.

***

Assistant Commissioner Alfred McDougall listened to undercover detective Sean Alderman intently.

Alderman had decided to set up the corrupt police officer, Michael Fagan and had engaged the support of detective

Colin Walker. To McDougall, the plan sounded logical but he thought if there had been more support at the scene, the gunfire may not have occurred. Yet, as Alderman had pointed out, any additional presence would have been far too obvious and the opportunity would have been lost.

The death of Jack Bissen, whilst it would draw an internal enquiry, was at the hands of a corrupt officer, Sean's recordings proved that. Besides, McDougall doubted that any adverse publicity in this case would result. He was sure the Emergency Services minister, Justin Kale, would be empathetic towards what had taken place, considering what had befallen his son.

McDougall had been pondering the situation for the past fifteen minutes since hanging up from Alderman. He had given Alderman free reign and whilst a fatality was regrettable, he considered stopping the corruption within the force was paramount.

Furthermore, in McDougall's mind, the death of Jacob Travis Bissen should be seen as a community god-send.

He picked up the phone and made the call he had promised to make. Vincent Cinelli picked up on the third ring.

***

Chapter Thirty-six

Lauren did indeed arrive home before Eileen was due to be dropped off. Actually she was home an hour earlier than expected. Time enough for a shower and change of clothes, into jeans and a short-sleeved top.

Lauren was looking through pantry contents to determine what she was going to prepare for dinner for her daughter and guests, Alison and Tim. She chose spiral pasta. She already had mushrooms, beans and peas that she had bought from the grocer the day before, and a chicken breast ready to chop and cook.

Lauren was surprised when the doorbell chimed. Both Eileen and Alison, for that matter, had keys. Then she realised it was half hour too early for them to arrive.

On opening the door, she was stunned to be facing two uniformed police officers with very grim faces. She automatically thought the worst.

"Where's Eileen, what's happened?" she gasped.

"Please, Ms Black, it is Ms Black, isn't it?" asked the policewoman, glancing sideways to her male counterpart.

"Yes, what's happened? Is Eileen alright?"

"We're not here about Eileen, so relax," said the male counterpart.

"We have to advise you that your ex-husband, Jacob Travis Bissen, is dead," said the policewoman formally.

"What? What do you mean, dead?" said Lauren, trying to

come to grips with what was unfolding. A wave of relief that Eileen was alright, followed immediately by a wave of shock, churned her stomach.

"I am Senior Constable Jones and my colleague here is Constable Warner. May we come in, Ms Black?" asked Jones. There was no doubt she was the one in charge.

"Yes, please come in, and please call me Lauren," said Lauren, feeling her head spin.

"I'm sorry, but you gave me a shock... I was expecting my daughter anytime now..." Lauren stammered.

"Totally, understandable, Lauren. We have not meant to cause alarm," said Jones.

Lauren sat down at the kitchen bench but did not invite the police officers to do so.

"Your ex-husband was killed this afternoon," said Jones evenly. She waited for a reaction.

"How?" asked Lauren.

For Lauren this was yet another horrifying out-of-body experience that she had endured because of her ex-husband.

"He was shot by a police officer," Constable Warner said, speaking for the first time since entering the house.

"That's yet to be substantiated, Lauren," cautioned Jones, glaring at her colleague.

"What happened?" asked Lauren, slowing gaining composure.

"We believe your husband.." said Warner.

"*Ex*-husband," interjected Lauren emphatically.

"Sorry, ex-husband," continued Warner.

"Your ex-husband was involved with numerous petty thefts, life endangerment and distribution of drugs."

"Officers, nothing surprises me about my ex," said Lauren, now gaining next to full composure.

"We were instructed to advise you of his death, Lauren," said Jones, her voice full of empathy.

"But why?" asked Lauren. "Surely you know he doesn't live here."

"You had a restraining order against your husband, sorry, your ex-husband, so this closes that loop," Warner explained, as though it was mere bureaucracy.

"Oh. Well, thanks for letting me know, I think," said Lauren.

A long moment of silent awkwardness took place and Lauren suggested they could show themselves out. She sat staring at her kitchen bench and then, as if moving on auto-pilot, started chopping beans and mushrooms.

It wasn't until she nicked her finger with the point of the knife and blood flowed, that she really took in the full significance of the police officers' visit.

Her ex-husband was dead.

This was the man who had slapped her only four or five days ago. She suddenly felt empty but knew she would have to have a discussion with her daughter; after all, the mongrel was her father. It was all so surreal.

She absently placed her cut finger in her mouth to stem the flow of blood and then put a band-aid on the cut. Her head was starting to pound, her anxiety level rising. *What do I say to Eileen?*

She didn't have time to think as Eileen came bustling in, with Alison and Tim following.

"Hi Mum," said Eileen.

"Hi Eils," her mother responded, grabbing her daughter and pulling her into a tight hug.

Alison could sense something was wrong and so could Eileen.

"What's up Mum? What's wrong?" Eileen pushed, her young face creased with concern.

Lauren gave a weak smile, acknowledging her daughter's perceptiveness.

"We need to talk," said Lauren.

Alison indicated that she and Tim could leave which Lauren quickly dismissed.

"No, stay Alison. I've already started prepping dinner," said Lauren, almost begging.

"So what's going on, mum?" Eileen persisted.

"It's about your father, Eileen," Lauren faltered.

"What about him? Has he been here again? Has he hurt you?" demanded Eileen with anger in her voice.

"No, Eileen, your father is dead."

"How?" asked Eileen, unflinching.

"He was shot by the police... I really don't know the details, but you know he was not a good man. In fact, he was really a very sick man and a drug addict."

Lauren waited for a reaction from her daughter. Alison and Tim remained quiet, frozen at the news.

"Good riddance," said Eileen finally.

"Eileen, he was still your father," Lauren couldn't help saying.

"No, he wasn't. He never did anything for me. He was no father."

Lauren knew these words to be true.

"The main thing, Mum, is are you alright?" Eileen asked quietly.

"That was going to be my question," interjected Alison. "Bloody hell!"

"Yes, I am fine. Let me finish prepping dinner. Alison, let's have a wine. You kids do your homework and then watch some television," said Lauren, giving herself a shake.

She was surprised how stoic, supportive and adult her daughter had been.

Chapter Thirty-seven

Lauren was happy to wake up with no hangover the next morning. She was even more pleased that Eileen was up and ready for school. The night before had finished well, and their friends had left before nine o'clock.

She had thought of Jack Bissen a few times throughout the night, but she knew that Eileen had been right; her former husband had caused nothing but misery and grief.

The police officers had told her that it would be quite some days before the body was released for burial, but she had made up her mind during the night that she would have nothing to do with it.

Firstly, she couldn't afford the expense of a funeral and secondly, she would feel like a hypocrite considering their last interaction less than a week ago, baseball bat included. She realised that she had grieved over the loss of her husband a long time ago and that was enough.

The best thing she could do was to get on with her work and she did not want to lose the momentum she believed she had struck up with Des Jamieson. She had plenty of work to do with her other patients as well. For that reason, after seeing both Eileen and Tim off to school, she was content to be sitting in her office reviewing the morning case files.

Jamieson's file notes hadn't changed that much, except for the small notation that he was becoming more fatigued, although he still made phone calls at odd hours and his lawyer continued to visit.

Lauren wondered how much money Vincent Cinelli was being paid. Her cynicism extended to the likelihood he was getting paid for every chess move and she knew how laboriously slow such moves could be. Chess had been something her mother had taught her when she was young, although she never matched her mother's winning standards.

When she arrived at Des Jameson's room, she was pleasantly surprised that the lawyer was not there and her patient was alone, soaking up the sun in the small garden courtyard. She did note a couple of pieces had been moved off the chessboard, indicating, as the report notes had informed, that Mr Cinelli had indeed visited.

"Good morning, Des," said Lauren as she sat down at the mosaic-covered table in the courtyard.

"Good morning, Lauren," said Des, his expression somewhat glum.

Lauren could easily tell something was on his mind but didn't push it at the onset.

"Do you want to do more letters?" Lauren asked.

"Sure, I think we can knock Fiona off the list and then my son, Ryan," he said.

"Fiona; she was your stepdaughter when you were married to Vivian, correct?"

"That's right."

"Do you think she will be receptive as I understand your divorce was … difficult?"

"Yes, it was. You've been doing your research."

"Well..."

"You are probably right in that she will not be receptive, but I did my best to be a father to her, so I should set a few things straight," he said emphatically.

Lauren could tell his spirits had significantly dropped since the last time she had seen Desmond. Something else was clearly wrong.

"Is there anything else troubling you, Des?"

"No, what's happening in your world, Lauren?" he deflected her question.

Lauren hesitated but it just spilled out.

"I told you about my ex-husband, remember? Well, he's dead."

"I'm sorry to hear that, Lauren."

"Don't be. In fact, it was my daughter, Eileen, who snapped me out of it. She reminded me of the sick person he was. She said that he had never been her father and she was right. He caused nothing but pain and grief and misery for a lot of people and especially me, as you know."

"I see, so you're OK with his passing?"

"Yes, I am, actually. I am just fine. So shall we get started?" posed Lauren, indicating the iPad she held in her hand. A weight seemed to fall from her shoulders.

"OK, jumping to electronic today, I see."

"Will be far more efficient."

"OK, let's do it; this will be short and sweet – 'Dear Fiona, it's been many years since I have seen you and I hope you are well. The reason I am writing to you is to advise you that I am not so well. In fact, I am dying. I always understood your loyalty to your mother. However, I have always acted in your best interests and tried my hardest to be the father you needed. Perhaps, not the father you wanted, but needed. If anything, I gave you too much attention and fulfilled all things you wanted. I hope, when you yourself one day have children of your own, you will put aside the selfish traits that have been inbred into you from your mother. Have a good life, your former step-father, Desmond Jamieson.'"

"Wow, you really are angry with her," said Lauren, rapidly tapping at the screen.

"If you think it needs softening, please do so but I hate to think how much I spoilt the girl and how she will grow up," said Desmond.

"No, that's OK. If that is how you feel?"

"I don't know where they are living. They sold the house I left for them in the divorce."

"You're telling me this is another letter that won't be sent?"

"Not trying to waste your valuable time, Lauren, and I have no intention of writing to Fiona's mother, as I would be a lot harsher. If you can find her, then we can send the letter."

"And what about your son, Ryan, or is that another letter that won't be sent?"

"No, indeed that letter must go out as soon as possible. You will find him in the next-of-kin details in my file along with Vincent's details."

"Are you going to write to Vincent as well?" Lauren asked in a tongue-in-cheek way.

"No need; I am taking care of Vincent separately."

Lauren could tell that Desmond was troubled and not in the right mood for her humour.

"OK, do you want to write your letter to Ryan now or do you need to rest?" asked Lauren.

"No, let's do it now if that's OK with you?"

"OK," agreed Lauren, opening a new page on her iPad.

Des cleared his throat as if again, he had already rehearsed what he wanted to convey.

"To my dear son, Ryan,

I hope this finds you well and all is going well in your world. Some months ago, I had extensive treatment for cancer. Unfortunately, it has come back with a vengeance and it is no longer treatable. I am currently in ResiCare and no doubt will be placed in PalCare in the very near future. I am so very sorry that I didn't spend more time with you in recent years and I am sorry that my work has taken me away so much of the time. On my passing, you will be notified by Vincent Cinelli who will advise you of my last will and testament. There is little more to say but how sorry I am in missing so many opportunities to be with you. Please know that I have always loved you, son. Love, Dad."

Lauren looked up from the iPad and could see tears welling in her patient's eyes.

"What else can I do for you, Des?"

"Nothing, thank you Lauren. I am suddenly feeling very weary," said Des, as he stood up with the drip trolley and rolled it back towards his bedroom.

"I will print out the letters and bring them to you to check later," she replied, with a tear suddenly springing to her eye.

"Thanks Lauren," said Des.

***

Back in her office, Lauren connected the iPad to her printer. She pondered over the conversation with Desmond. Had he been troubled because of the letters he had dictated; the one to Fiona or Ryan or both?

But why was he so blunt when she first sat down? Going over the discussion in her mind, she realised he had again gotten her to talk about her personal life. Again it had been about her ex-husband and this time it was about his death.

He had said, 'I am sorry to hear that, Lauren,' but he never asked about how Jack Bissen had died. Perhaps he just assumed it was due to drugs? But what had he said a few days ago when she told him about her horrific time with her ex-husband? Then it came to her; he had said, *'I want to make sure he doesn't worry you again.'*

Surely not. Surely he could not have had anything to do with Jack's death. It had to be coincidental. Anyway, she had other patients to visit plus a new patient that had been added to her list that had to be on-boarded.

She took the letters off the printer and decided she would see Desmond later and ask him straight out. Suddenly, it was looking like it was going to be a long day. She picked up the phone and called her mother to let her know that she might be running late and that Eileen would be coming to her and she would pick her daughter up as soon as possible.

She had called her mother late last night after Alison and Tim had left, and told her of the police officers' visit about

Jack. Her mother's response had been very gentle.

"I'm so sorry, Lauren. That must have been a horrible shock. It sounds like it's for the best, and that Eileen knows that." Lauren found herself nodding. Deep down, it was only Eileen's reaction that mattered.

It was six in the evening by the time Lauren got back to Desmond's room, with the two letters in hand. He was awake but only just, so this was not the time to raise her thoughts with him about her dead ex-husband.

"I have the letters, Des, and I noted Ryan's email address in your file so once you check it, I can email it out," said Lauren quietly.

"It's OK Lauren, I trust you; just send it," said Desmond, wearily, his eyes almost closed.

"Is there anyone else I can reach out to, for you?"

"Yes, I want to find Kes," he said, his voice barely audible

"Kez? Who is Kez?"

"My first true love... Kes."

And with that Desmond Jamieson closed his eyes and was asleep.

Chapter Thirty-eight

As Lauren drove towards her mother's house, she was totally confused. She had emailed the letter to Ryan Jamieson with a mental note to call him tomorrow and follow up, but Des Jamieson had never mentioned a Kez. She wasn't even sure of the spelling but phonetically, that's how it sounded. Unless he gave her more information, or if his son could shed some light on this, it was going to be impossible. Nothing in her research had come up with anything like Kez.

Theresa was on reception duty but on the phone when she had left the hospital. She gave the hand and finger signal between ear and mouth, indicating for Theresa to call her as soon as possible.

She was just putting the key into the front door of her mother's house when Theresa returned her call. She walked through to the kitchen where her mother and daughter were sitting at the table. She put her finger to her lips and went to the back family room.

"Hi Theresa, I need an eye kept on Desmond Jamieson, room 314," said Lauren.

"Sure Lauren, anything in particular?" said Theresa.

"Well just before fatigue set in, he mentioned the name 'Kez' but that's all I got. I'm not sure if it was Kez or how to spell it. If he wakes I need more information."

"You mean Kes, like in "A Kestrel for a Knave"?"

"What?"

"It was yet another high school book I was supposed to have read."

"That's funny, but I don't think he is wanting a bird of prey," said Lauren.

"I'll keep an eye and ear out."

"Thanks Theresa, give me a call if needed."

Lauren walked back to the kitchen where her mother was standing behind the bench.

"What's up Mum, you look a little pale?" asked Lauren.

"Just a little tired, didn't sleep well last night. Nothing to worry about," replied Caitlin.

"Are we going home now, Mum?" asked Eileen.

"Yes, we are. Where's your school bag?"

"Right here," said Eileen, picking up the bag laden with schoolbooks.

Eileen gave her grandmother a kiss as did Lauren and they were out the door and on their way home.

Chapter Thirty-nine

Desmond Jamieson was drifting in and out of sleep. The pain was on the increase and he pushed the regulator to increase the flow. He knew he was on the decline and most likely heading for PalCare as early as tomorrow if not even tonight.

His bedside lamp was on but the main light in his room was off. The door was open when the hallucinations started, with someone silhouetted in the doorway.

Then someone was holding his hand and he felt a kiss to his forehead and then his lips. The person spoke softly as he continued to open and close his eyes. He was struggling to make sense of everything the voice was saying, and then the soft voice in the darkness promised to return. Then there was nothing.

He went back to dozing but that voice was resounding in his mind. He sat up, turned the dimmer switch up to provide more light, and picked up his mobile.

"Desmond, what is it?" asked Vincent Cinelli.

"I have one last job for you, Vincent," said Desmond.

Fifteen minutes later Des hung up the phone. He reached for the bedside drawer and took out a writing pad and pen. He feverishly started to write, controlling his shaking hand as much as possible. This was one letter he was destined to write himself.

Then nature called and he knew he had to go to the bathroom. Damn, why now? He thought of pressing the buzzer for a bottle to be delivered but then he thought better of it. He didn't want the nursing staff interfering and suggesting he stop working.

Get up Desmond, walk to the ensuite and then finish the letter.

He carefully got out of bed to make sure the drip trolley stayed upright and walked to the ensuite.

Chapter Forty

It was six in the morning when Lauren's mobile rang. She was already up for the day, had showered and dressed. She was hoping she would get more information out of Des Jamieson. The mystery of Kes was filling her mind. He had referred to her as his true love.

How many women in one lifetime had he known?

She answered the phone and when she heard the voice of Amelia Schwartz, she knew it couldn't be good news.

"Lauren, can you get to the office as soon as possible?" said the CEO without preamble.

"What's wrong, Amelia? Is it Des Jamieson?" asked Lauren.

"Yes, but I need to see you. We have matters to discuss. I'll see you soon," said Amelia, hanging up the phone.

Lauren was dumbfounded. Had Des told Amelia about her divulging her personal life? It was probably a breach of all protocols but then, Amelia had said in an email, to keep doing what she was doing.

Lauren phoned Alison and asked her to do the school run, saying she had an urgent call to go to the hospital. On arrival, instead of reporting to Amelia Schwartz's office, she headed straight to room 314, Des Jamieson's room. Sitting on the chair at the small table was Amelia, looking dismal. The chess board was nowhere in sight, and nor was Des Jamieson. The room seemed bare and cold without his presence.

"Has he been taken to PalCare?" asked Lauren.

"No, Lauren, he had a heart attack late last night and didn't survive. Theresa found him in the bathroom," said Amelia.

"No, no, no. I hadn't finished what he asked of me," said Lauren, collapsing into the seat opposite Amelia.

"I think you did, but may not know it," said Amelia, handing over a folded piece of paper.

Lauren took the page with handwritten scrawl but the letter stopped midway.

It read:

> *Dearest Lauren,*
>
> *Thank you for all you have done and what a miracle you have been. You sent my Kes to me. I am so sorry, I didn't know I had a daughter for all of these years. I would never have left. I would have stayed and fought if I knew you were going to be born. Now, I find I have a granddaughter in Eileen as well. I hope I can now meet her.*
>
> *I never stopped loving your mother and I should have realised you were her daughter. You share the same beauty and now I recall that fragrance.*
>
> *You must trust Vincent when I am gone as I intend to ensure you are looked after.*
>
> *I wish that*

That's where the letter finished. Lauren jumped up and ran to the ward reception desk and there in the visitor book was the name Kes, but the 'K' had the familiar flourish of her mother's handwriting.

She went back to the room, tears in her eyes.

"I don't understand," she stammered.

"I didn't know, Lauren, I promise. What can I do for you?" asked Amelia.

"How could he be my father – my father died years ago, what on earth is going on here?"

Then a sudden and familiar voice came from the doorway behind them.

"He's gone, hasn't he?" said Lauren's mother.

Lauren spun around, anger flushing her cheeks.

"I think you two need some time to talk," said Amelia.

"Too right, Amelia," said Lauren. "Come with me," she snapped at her mother, who followed her daughter down the corridor and into Lauren's office.

Lauren took her seat behind the desk and motioned her mother to sit in one of the visitor chairs.

"Why have you lied to me all my life?" Lauren demanded, shaking, tears running down her cheeks.

"It was to protect you," said her mother, beginning to sob as well.

"Bullshit, Mum. You told me my father was dead."

"In many regards, he was. If you can be quiet for just a moment, I will tell you how Des' life, and my life, has played out," said Caitlin, brushing tears away.

"Go on," said Lauren, unsure where to direct the tumultuous anger and confusion she was feeling inside.

"I truly loved Des with all my heart. Unfortunately, and this is going to sound terrible but at that time, there was another suitor."

Lauren frowned, not just because the word *suitor* was so oddly old-fashioned, but she suddenly had an image of her mother being a wild party girl and a promiscuous one at that. *Surely, my mother wasn't a slut.*

"My father was hell-bent on me marrying Bill. Absolutely hated Desmond, regardless of how much Des tried," continued Caitlin, her voice aching with sadness.

"Des was more chivalrous than I could give him credit for. He knew I was being torn apart so he proposed to me, but my father's voice was too loud in my mind and I turned down the proposal. The greatest mistake and loss of my life.

"He transferred to Brisbane the very next day and by the time I had realised I was pregnant with you, he had already moved to South East Asia. I tried to get in contact but it was impossible. He was moving around so much.

"My father, your grandfather, insisted I have an abortion and then marry Bill."

"How did you know I wasn't Bill's daughter," asked Lauren, her voice still bristling with indignation.

"Simple, dear – I had never slept with Bill," Caitlin replied with a small lift of her shoulders.

"Go on," said Lauren, chastened.

"So, regardless of my father's persistence, and the fact that I adored my father, I made a very clear decision to leave home and for my parents never to find me."

"That must have been very hard," acknowledged Lauren.

"Yes, it was. It was heartbreaking but not as heartbreaking as losing Des. My mistake. They were some very big decisions to make. I was so young and I have regretted my mistake for all my life.

"I followed Des' climb to business fame. Fame, an interesting word, as I have never known anyone as humble and sensible as Desmond Jamieson.

"Anyway, I left home. I had to work hard, knowing I was going to have a baby; you were growing inside of me. I changed my name from Karen Eileen Swanson."

"K.E.S. - Kes," said Lauren.

"That's right; Des always referred to me as Kes," said Caitlin, more tears slowly trickling down her face.

Lauren handed her mother the tissue box sitting atop of her desk, which Caitlin accepted, dabbing at her cheeks, willing them to be dry.

"I followed your father's career. I was in the hope I would reconnect one day but then I saw the news on the internet. Yes, another lie, Lauren; I have always been computer literate. He had married a Chinese businesswoman," Caitlin added, her head bowed.

"Janice Lee," replied Lauren, nodding.

"Yes, Janice Lee. That was her name. My understanding is that she passed away not long after their marriage."

"She died giving birth to a baby girl and the baby was lost also," explained Lauren, feeling again the sorrow from the letter Des had dictated only some days ago.

"That's terrible; I never knew. Anyway, I continued to watch out for Des and ultimately he remarried at least twice more," Caitlin continued.

"I told you your father was dead and yes, that was so wrong of me. I was living the lie. I didn't want to intrude on whatever happiness he was having, and I know that sounds strange, but he taught me so much.

"That's why I told you how wonderful he was when you were a child. He taught me how to love and laugh. He is - was, a beautiful soul. When we worked together, he wrote me prose; such beautiful prose, nearly every day," said the half-sobbing Caitlin.

"It's hard to believe, as he was such a powerhouse businessman but then I have seen his emotions and caring. If he had known where you were, he would have written a letter that was so beautiful. That I am sure about," said Lauren.

"I'm sorry Lauren. Can you forgive me?" asked Caitlin. Her voice wavered, pain threaded through her tears.

"I will. I just wish I had known but then again, I wouldn't have been his carer." Lauren sighed heavily. "Maybe I would have gotten to know him in a different time and way, and we would have been here visiting together every day."

"That's true but I had lost touch. He could have been anywhere in the world."

"Yes, but how did you find out he was here now? Did you overhear me on the phone last night?"

"Yes, that's why I said I was tired and needed you and Eileen to go home. I heard you say Des Jamieson and there are a thousand Desmond Jamiesons in this world, I can tell you that."

Lauren nodded, knowing that only too well, having done her online research.

"But then I heard you say *Kes*, and I knew; it was my Des you were talking about," concluded Caitlin.

There was silence for a few moments, and then Caitlin spoke again.

"I hope I didn't precipitate his passing. Please tell me that's not the case," she said, pleading.

"No, I don't believe so but he was in a very big rush to write this letter so he may have been overexerting," said Lauren, who still had the letter firmly in her grip.

"We picked up a small heart murmur a few days ago and he was getting weaker by the hour," added Lauren, handing the letter to her mother.

Caitlin unfolded the letter and read the incomplete script, and her tears started to cascade all over again.

Lauren reached into her desk drawer and retrieved the bottle of brandy and two tumblers. She slowly poured a decent two fingers full measure and handed one of them to her mother.

Chapter Forty-one

The funeral of Desmond Allen Jamieson was held at the non-denominational chapel at Fawkner Cemetery where he was to be later cremated.

Lauren and Eileen picked up Caitlin Black, aka Karen Eileen Swanson, to attend the service. They had plenty of time, so they sat around the kitchen table where Caitlin had laid out two scrap books full of media clippings that involved Desmond Jamieson.

Eileen had been told by her mother of her deceased grandfather and the circumstances as retold by her grandmother, and was saddened to not have known her grandfather. However, Eileen was stoic, a trait that ran through her mother and grandmother.

Caitlin then produced the red hard-covered Collins feint-lined book, handing it to Lauren.

Lauren opened the book, to see page after page of prose written by Desmond Jamieson. She was overwhelmed by the beauty and potency of some of the written pieces. The handwriting was clear and firm, unlike the scrawl that filled the incomplete letter at the hospital.

Some of the prose had a one-line comment in her mother's handwriting and it was so obvious that this young couple from long ago were so in love. She could not help but think, *How tragic for us all.*

They drove to the cemetery and on arrival at the chapel, it appeared to be standing room only, with more than two hundred in attendance. Some mourners had to stand outside while the three of them were ushered to the front right pew that was reserved for them.

There was a man standing to the left of the pulpit talking to a woman dressed in a pale yellow skirt and matching jacket. The word *canary* came fleetingly to mind but Lauren assumed her to be the celebrant. She hadn't a clue who the man might be, until he turned his head. He was tall, thin but well built, with dark hair and a smile she immediately recognised. This had to be Ryan Jamieson, her stepbrother.

To the left in the adjacent pew, was none other than Vincent Cinelli. What had her father's letter to her said? *You must trust Vincent when I am gone as I intend to ensure you are looked after.*

Next to Vincent, who was dressed impeccably in a dark, expensive three-piece pinstriped suit, was a striking man of Asian appearance. She had no idea who he might be but thought his appearance bizarre. The man had silver hair; the most silver of hair she had ever seen, along with a thin pencil-line of a moustache and whispery stripe of hair that formed a line from just under his bottom lip to the end of his chin. *Who comes to a funeral in a pure white, silk suit?*

However, that was not the only unusual thing she was to discover about this funeral service, as the first music was now resounding around the chapel; *As time goes by.* Her mother actually had a smile on her face, as she silently mouthed the words in unison with the recording.

Ryan Jamieson left the celebrant behind at the pulpit, indicating proceedings were about to begin, as the final chorus sounded; *As time goes by.* Ryan walked across the floor to Lauren, bent down and whispered to her.

"You must be Lauren, I am Ryan. We can talk later, if you like. Thank you for the letter," he softly said, and took her hand with a gentle shake.

Lauren just nodded, and agreed, thinking, *I have no idea what it's like to have a brother.* It was bizarre to meet a person who shared half her DNA, yet was a total stranger. Ryan sat down beside her. Next to Lauren was her mother and next to her mother was Eileen.

The celebrant, a petite woman, bent the microphone down to her mouth level and spoke for the first time.

"Good morning everyone. My name is Anna Tobias and I am a celebrant recognised by both State and Federal law. I am here to welcome you all for the celebration of the life of Desmond Allen Jamieson. However, as Desmond has given instructions through his lawyer, this is going to be a lazy morning for me, as I need say very little," the celebrant said emphatically.

"Instead, I am going to ask for a couple of guest speakers along, with any family member present if they wish to contribute to this celebration of Desmond's life. Not just his life but his love for life. You will note there is no coffin and again that has been one of Desmond's wishes. He has said, this is 'a time for loved ones to party' quote, unquote.

"Desmond has chosen some songs he would like played during this short service. You have just heard, *As time goes by,* which was evidently important to him and I am sure, reflective of a loving memory. So now can the second number be played please, followed by an address by Mr Cinelli," she concluded.

Lauren was expecting Amazing Grace but thought that would be at the end of the service: perhaps Psalm 23, *The Lord is my shepherd,* but no; Johnny Cash's voice echoed through the chapel with *Burning ring of fire.* Now she knew she was unlikely to second guess anything about this service.

As the music came to a stop, Vincent Cinelli came to the pulpit. He had no more than two pages which he rested there. *Still charging by the minute,* thought Lauren but she dismissed the request in her father's letter. In reality, she was still coming to grips that she actually had a father in Desmond Jamieson.

Vincent, being much taller than the celebrant, raised the microphone and looked out to the audience.

"Good morning. I see a number of faces I recognise but for those who do not know me, my name is Vincent Cinelli," he said.

"Firstly, please allow me to express my condolences to Desmond's family who are present; his son, Ryan, daughter, Lauren, and granddaughter, Eileen, but more so to the woman he never fell out of love with, Caitlin, or should I say, Karen as Desmond knew her. When he spoke of Karen, he always referred to her as Kes."

Lauren was almost alarmed, while her mother gave a small sniffle. Vincent nodded to those sitting in the first pew and then continued.

"I have known Desmond Jamieson for more than twenty years. I have been his lawyer; at times, business partner; confidante and much more. Desmond has been my closest and dearest friend and I will miss him dearly.

"It is true to say, I have made my fortune thanks to Desmond, but he has never paid me a cent. Instead, he has opened many doors to other clients; some of whom are here today."

Lauren flushed, ashamed. *You must trust Vincent...*

"For those who knew Desmond, you would know his financial and auditing skills were second to none. His strategic business mind was also second to none. He played business hard, but he was also fair.

"His compassion for others was second to none as well. He once said to me something to the effect, *Doing good business also means giving back,* or something like that. He lived by this belief. It was his motto. He established philanthropic trusts, supported and raised funds for many worthy causes, including the hospital where he finally passed away, three days ago."

Vincent's eyes were watering, and his voice had started to quaver.

"To conclude, I have a few more duties to perform for Desmond involving his family. I will miss our many chess battles, which by the way, Desmond invariably won. I will miss you, my friend. Rest in peace," said Vincent, wiping his eyes and returning to his seat.

Lauren's eyes were misty to say the least. She held her mother's hand tightly, while Ryan placed his hand on her shoulder momentarily as a sign of comfort to his new-found stepsister. Caitlin remained misty-eyed, discarding her usual stoic manner. Then the music started again; this time, *What I did for love*. It was the old Johnny Mathis version, and Lauren felt as if Johnny himself was in the chapel. The three held hands and smiled.

Again, as if rehearsed, the music stopped and this time, the man in the white suit rose from his seat and went to the pulpit. This time, there was no need to adjust the microphone, suggesting he was similar in height to Vincent. Lauren couldn't help but notice how impeccably he was dressed, just as Vincent Cinelli was, but all in white. Everything in fact, was in white, including his matching tie and shoes.

"My name is William Chen. I have known Desmond since the early days of his career and he has been very effective in many audits, transactions and negotiations for my company. I have appreciated the counsel he has provided and beyond business, he has been a good friend.

"Today, I am pledging two million Australian dollars to the ResiCare and PalCare facilities at City General in perpetuity."

He looked towards Vincent, who was holding three fingers across his chest.

"Sorry, I meant three million Australian dollars, in perpetuity. Thank you. Rest in peace, Desmond," concluded Chen.

Lauren glanced back to see Amelia Schwartz two rows behind her and she looked both startled and happy at the same time.

As Chen went back to his seat, which was obviously the cue, music started again. John Paul Young's *Love is in the air* echoed around the chapel. The realisation dawned on Lauren that Desmond was playing all of her mother's old favourites; the tunes and lyrics that Lauren had grown up with. They shared a smile of incredulity and recognition. There would be no Amazing Grace today.

In fact, much of this ceremony was not a celebration of Desmond's life. Lauren believed it to be more of a tribute to her mother.

At the conclusion of the song, Anna Tobias was once again behind the pulpit, lowering the microphone.

"I ask if anyone else would like to say a few words, then please step forward. Ryan you have already expressed to me your love for your father but have chosen not to speak. Does anyone else want to contribute?" said Anna.

Lauren looked at her mother, who gave a tiny shake of her head. She could see her mother now becoming more distraught, losing her normal confident, polished air.

Lauren, mind made up, raised her hand, which the celebrant acknowledged, and Lauren stepped forward. Behind the pulpit she raised the microphone once more.

She hadn't planned to say anything but her own emotions were screaming inside of her. She took a deep breath.

"I was Desmond's carer in ResiCare, so I am very grateful for Mr Chen's generosity," said Lauren.

Chen nodded his head in acknowledgement. She then took another deep breath.

"I didn't know Desmond Jamieson for very long. In fact, I didn't know he was my father until three days ago. I didn't know that I had a stepbrother and I am very pleased, Ryan, you were able to make it here today, all the way from Darwin.

"Life takes many twists and turns and sometimes, those twists and turns don't take us where life should. I believe I am very good at my job and often see the best and the worst in patients as they make their way to that final destination.

"My boss, Amelia, is here today and she knew my father well; not well enough to know that he was my father but then again, my father didn't know he had a daughter, either. But Amelia warned me of this headstrong patient I was taking on; that he would be stubborn; he would be controlling to the end.

"Amelia was right. However, Desmond and I struck a chord and I started to see this tough businessman, who had worked hard all his life, show his true colours; shades of compassion and kindness.

"I will always wonder what my life would have been like, if my father had been a part of it. I have been very fortunate to have had a wonderful mother who nurtured my growth. Ironically, what I have learnt from my mother over the years has been well supplemented with the knowledge I have gained in the short time I have spent with Desmond. Thank you," said Lauren, returning to the open arms of her mother.

"Thank you, Lauren; that was beautifully said. Thank you all for your attendance, and Mr Cinelli and Mr Chen for your contributions. Can we please stand for one minute's final silence and think on what Desmond Jamieson has meant to each of us and pray for him in our own way," Anna Tobias said.

Lauren always hated that awkward moment of silence and was relieved when the celebrant spoke again.

"Desmond Allen Jamieson, we wish you well in the next stage of your journey, knowing you will be missed and knowing how much love is in this chapel today. May you rest in peace. Ladies and gentlemen, thank you again for your attendance. That concludes our service here today," said Anna Tobias.

As is the norm with such ceremonies, people started to leave from the front pews first. As Lauren and her mother stood up to exit, a final song came through the speakers. It was the Commodores with Lionel Richie singing *Three times a lady*. Caitlin started to stagger and Lauren thought she was going to faint so she took her mother by the arm to support her walk up the aisle.

"That's the one special thing about your father, Lauren. He always defended me to my critics or anyone making a snide comment about our affairs; he always called me a lady," Caitlin said softly.

Outside the chapel, many that had been standing outside, taking in the service through external speakers, were already beginning to disperse. There were, however, a number of well-wishers who came up to both Lauren and Ryan, to express their condolences. Caitlin and Eileen stood back, even though a few approached Caitlin.

Lauren couldn't help but think how strange it was that none of the well-wishers were known to any of them, but that's the way it is. Peoples' way of paying their final respects.

Amelia Schwartz waited in the background and finally drew near to give Lauren that same warm hug as she had in her office that day. She then gave Caitlin similar treatment; her eyes reddened by tears she had shed during the service.

Will Chen stepped forward to pay his respects and again Lauren thanked him for his generosity. She then took the opportunity to introduce Chen to Amelia.

"I have a car waiting Ms Schwartz; if I can offer you a ride, we can talk further about the good things you are doing at your hospital," offered Chen, courteously inclining his head.

"That would be lovely, Mr Chen, as I caught a taxi to get here, but please call me Amelia," she replied and the two walked off in the direction of the car park.

That left Caitlin, Lauren, Eileen and Ryan standing there talking, until Lauren noticed Vincent in the background, handing what looked like a cheque to the celebrant. Vincent then joined the four related individuals.

"Lauren, Caitlin; I'm sorry. Like you, I didn't know I had any relations," said Ryan.

"I can tell you all, albeit very late, that Desmond loved you all," interjected Vincent.

"Mr Cinelli, I have to apologise. I got you wrong; all so wrong," blurted out Lauren.

"I know, Lauren. You thought I was one of those money-hungry lawyers, like the ambulance chasers that bring the profession a bad name," said Vincent, with a knowing smile.

"Something like that," Lauren responded feebly.

"I know this is bad timing, but can I ask you all to attend my office tomorrow. There is the matter of Desmond's will," said Vincent, handing out business cards.

"Sure, I have to get back home to Darwin as soon as I can. Tomorrow is fine," said Ryan.

"That's fine with us as well, although I don't believe we are expecting anything," said Lauren.

"Good, I'll explain everything tomorrow. Can we say nine, tomorrow morning?" said Vincent, not waiting for an answer but instead turning away and heading for the car park.

"Nine it is, then," said Ryan, his smile so oddly familiar.

Chapter Forty-two

The drive home from Fawkner Cemetery had been a quiet one. Lauren and Caitlin had been deep in thought. Ryan had taken a taxi to the hotel where he was staying. Caitlin declined Lauren's offer to stay with her and Eileen for the night.

"Are you sure, Mum? It's been such a big day and I need to know you will be alright," said Lauren.

"I'm fine, thanks Lauren, but if you could pick me up tomorrow to go to Mr Cinelli's office, that would be good. Pointless taking two cars and paying for two lots of parking," Caitlin had replied.

The morning came after restless nights for both Lauren and her mother, but Lauren and Eileen were there as requested, having picked up Caitlin, then driving to Vincent Cinelli's office.

On arrival, they found Ryan already there, sitting in the waiting area. Lauren signed in on behalf of her mother and daughter and the receptionist asked them to take a seat.

"Good morning," said Ryan, who also looked bleary-eyed from lack of sleep.

"Good morning," said Lauren and Caitlin, almost in unison, while Eileen gave a simple, "Hi."

Ryan explained he had only arrived just before them and that he had his flight home mid-afternoon.

It was exactly 9am when the door to Vincent's office swung open and Vincent greeted them, ushering them in.

The office was quite sizable with an impressive view of the bay, a large mahogany desk one end, and a matching round table at the other, along with padded leather seats.

Vincent offered to arrange for tea and coffee, as he invited them all to sit around the table. They declined so instead Vincent poured glasses of water that rested on a silver tray on the table in front of them.

Vincent then also sat down, unpacking a folder which contained three documents, along with duplicate copies. He placed the relevant titled documents in front of Ryan, Lauren and Caitlin, meticulously lining them up.

"Firstly, I need to explain what has taken place leading up to today. Ryan, this affects you more than anyone," said Vincent.

"It is unusual for a person's lawyer to have power of attorney but not out of the question, and as I explained at yesterday's service, your father has been much more than a mere client to me, and I to him.

"The night of his passing, he called me to make changes to his last will and testament. These changes are documented in front of you and you will all have time to read them.

"Ryan, you have every right to contest this will, but I will premise that by emphasising that these are his last directions to me and the will has been divided based on a larger cash inheritance to you, Ryan, and an equivalent share to be divided between you, Lauren and Caitlin. There has been a lesser amount placed in trust for Eileen, which she will be able to access at the age of twenty-five.

"Caitlin's share includes a property. This property is the only remaining property belonging to Desmond. All other assets have been sold prior to establishment of this will. It is Desmond's wish that this property may be handed down to her daughter or granddaughter, depending on who may depart this world first. However, legally that will depend on you, Caitlin.

"Before I continue, are there any questions on what I have imparted so far?"

All four looked at each other and shook their heads. Eileen followed suit as she hadn't a clue what this man was talking about. Lauren on the other hand was somewhat dumbfounded by the high level legal jargon. Ryan looked a little anxious but gave the appearance he was following the briefing, while Caitlin looked completely relaxed and if not, was showing her polished poker face.

"Good, I will continue," said the lawyer.

"Ryan, your inheritance equates to a net $12 million. Note, I said *net*. As we know, your father was a financial wizard and he has been able to pay all death duties and taxes already; an arrangement he negotiated with the tax office."

Ryan had paled instantly and appeared to be slightly trembling. The lawyer continued quickly.

"Ryan, knowing that both your legal stepmother and stepsister will share the same amount, do you intend to contest this will?" he asked the shaken Ryan.

"The amount is beyond my comprehension, but even if it was twelve dollars, I would not contest. These are my father's dying wishes," replied Ryan nervously.

Vincent nodded in approval, stood up and opened his office door, beckoning his receptionist to come in.

"That being the case, Ryan, can you please turn to page three of the document in front of you and sign the waiver where indicated," he directed Ryan.

Ryan did as he was instructed.

"Elsie, can you please witness Mr Jamieson's signature," said Vincent.

Elsie, the receptionist when they first arrived, was obviously used to witnessing such documents. She signed and then silently retreated back to her work area.

"Ryan, you are free to stay to hear the rest of the terms of the will or depart as you wish," said Vincent.

"No, I am happy to leave. My father had full confidence in

you for many years and I trust you equally. However, I would like to keep in touch with my *new family*, if that's alright," said Ryan, turning to Lauren and Caitlin.

"I think we would like that, Ryan," said Caitlin, breaking her silence for the first time since entering the lawyer's office. She gave him a warm smile and he smiled back, his expression so similar to Des'.

Kisses were exchanged and Ryan shook hands with Vincent, thanking him for all of his good work. He then left the office with a level of disbelief over what had just taken place.

"He is very much like his father in many ways," said Vincent.

"Yes, he is," said Caitlin.

"Let's continue, shall we? Lauren, you will receive $6 million net, with the same conditions that applied to Ryan. Any questions?" asked Vincent.

Lauren took the glass in front of her, her hand shaking, but managing to take a large gulp of water.

"Yes, I think so, but how could the same arrangements be made with the tax office when he had already died?" she asked.

"As power of attorney, I was able to forward the same documentation to the tax commissioner and that approval came through yesterday morning. The same applies to you Caitlin, but your inheritance equates to $2 million net plus one property," explained Vincent.

"That's one very expensive property, then. But believe me, I don't care. I am still reeling from reconnecting one day and losing Des again, the next," said Caitlin, letting out a deep breath.

"I understand, believe me. If you are both agreeable, I would ask you both to turn to page six of the documents in front of you and sign where indicated," said Vincent, again exiting to bring Elsie back in to witness.

Elsie again dutifully completed her witnessing task.

"Elsie, just stay one moment. There is one more document to be witnessed. Lauren, your father has entrusted you to ensure the trust deed in the name of your daughter is enacted when she turns 25. The amount of this trust currently sits at $2 million but is subject to growth over the ensuing years. Please sign page two of this document and Elsie will witness," he said, handing over the extra document.

"Job done. I know this is still a sad time, but I know Desmond will be pleased from above with how well everything has been handled." Vincent nodded with satisfaction as he neatly gathered the documents together.

"Copies of all documentation will be forwarded to you and funds will be transferred to your accounts by the end of next week. You should attain financial and investment advice to minimise further taxation, which interest on your accounts will attract.

"Now I have one more task to complete, so I would ask you to accompany me to the premises that Desmond has bequeathed to you, Caitlin. Is that alright?"

"Where is this property, Vincent?" asked Lauren, imaging some form of warehouse or factory.

"It's about 45 minutes away and I will be happy to drive you and then return you to where you have parked your car," replied Vincent.

There was assent from them all, so Vincent took one more file out of his filing cabinet and they took the lift to the basement where his car, a black Mercedes C series, was parked.

Again, there was little conversation during the drive, due to the mounting anticipation. Then, Caitlin began to recognise a few roads and when Vincent turned up a particular side road, she knew she had been here many years ago. The feeling grew stronger when Vincent turned up a long bitumen drive and there it was.

The house was not huge, but its modern design was ultra-impressive, with its well-appointed garden and large windows with spectacular views of both bays. Overcome with feeling, Caitlin almost fell getting out of the car, so she grabbed hold of Lauren's arm for support.

"Let's go in," said Vincent, holding up the keys in his hand.

When they entered, Caitlin, Lauren and Eileen were taken aback by its beauty. Lauren turned to her mother, who was pale and obviously emotional.

"Are you OK, Mum?" she asked.

"Your father brought me here when it was just empty land, years ago, and he said he would build me a house on this very spot. He and I fell in love with the views but at the time I didn't take him seriously, and yet, here it is," said Caitlin in wonder.

"But it's so modern; surely it can only be a few years old," said Lauren.

"Perhaps, I should explain," interjected Vincent.

The two women turned to face Vincent, while Eileen continued gazing out to the sea.

"When Desmond's wife Carol, Ryan's mother, had a stroke and was admitted to care in what can only be described as a vegetative state, Desmond was committed to making her as comfortable as possible, but he ultimately knew he had to let go.

"He bought this land some 20 years ago, but three years ago, he designed this house himself and contracted builders and here it is. He had the misguided belief he would find you, Kes, and he searched, never discovering how your life turned out or your change of name. You had disappeared off the face of the earth.

"So, he completed this house but then he contracted the first bout of cancer so now the rest is history," concluded Vincent.

"It's a beautiful home, just as I would have imagined it. However, it may be too large for me," said Caitlin.

"Not if you have boarders. I could live here," said Lauren enthusiastically, her eyes drinking in the splendour of the views.

"So, could I, Gran," said Eileen, weighing into the conversation.

"Well, that's all up to you, but I know Desmond would be proud. Here are the deeds," added Vincent, handing over an envelope.

"Well, sounds amazing, doesn't it. I just wish he was here," said Caitlin.

"Shall we head back after you've had a look around the house?" asked Vincent.

"Yes, by all means but could I have a quiet word with you Vincent?" asked Lauren, leading Vincent into the next large room, which was fully furnished and had an open fireplace.

"What's worrying you, Lauren?" asked Vincent, detecting something was troubling her.

"I have to ask you this, straight out. Did my father have anything to do with the death of Jack Bissen? He said he wanted to be sure he didn't bother me again," she asked in a hushed tone. Her green eyes watched him intently.

"No, definitely not. However, there was some coincidence. Your ex-husband was involved with a lot of drug deals and petty theft and he was paying off a very corrupt police officer. Desmond asked me to enquire about him, to keep you safe. We didn't know there was police corruption involved at the time. There was a stakeout involving two undercover cops. They arrested the corrupt officer but not before he had shot Jack Bissen, wounding him fatally," replied Vincent.

"Thanks, Vincent. I so much wanted to believe my father and you, for that matter, were not involved." Lauren felt an invisible weight fall from her shoulders.

"I understand, that's quite alright. Let's get you all back home," Vincent said, looking at his watch.

Eileen sat in the front passenger seat while Lauren and her mother sat in the back. Caitlin reached over and held her daughter's hand with a firm grip but was silent all the way back to where Lauren's car had been parked.

For Lauren and Caitlin, the entire experience had been nothing but surreal. There was all this new wealth but with it came a sense of inexplicable emptiness. The loss of what could have been.

As the trio disembarked from Vincent's car, they thanked him for all he had done. Vincent got out of the car and Lauren gave him a long, meaningful hug.

"My duties go beyond the grave. Des meant a lot to me. If there is anything I can do for any of you, please call me," said Vincent.

They parted ways and Vincent drove into his office building carpark. Taking the lift to the seventeenth floor, he entered the reception area. The building was empty; Elsie and the other staff had left for the day.

At that moment, Vincent also had an immense feeling of emptiness. There was a sadness building inside of him and he was feeling weary. Simply, he had not had time to grieve the loss of his closest friend.

On approaching his office door, he found it locked which was not unusual, as Elsie would do this in his absence for the sake of security. He took the key from his pocket and unlocked the door but on entering, he was taken by surprise.

There on the table was the beautifully adorned, marble chess board. The pieces were laid out exactly as they had been when they last played; a few pawns on the table that had been lost in the early stages of the battle. A tear came to his eye and his face crumpled. He could not understand how this could have happened.

Next to the chessboard was a simple envelope bulging in the middle. He opened it and removed what was a solid gold chess piece, a king, along with a note that read:

My dear friend Vincent,
You got me at last,
Checkmate.
Desmond

Epilogue

Caitlin did engage the services of Vincent Cinelli, a mere week after their parting, and through his guidance she altered her own last will and testament.

Vincent was not surprised that Kes wanted to leave the *Two Bays* property to Lauren, along with her current family home. What did take him by surprise was the two million dollars she wished to donate to the facility that was caring for Desmond's ex-wife and Ryan's mother, Carol.

When asked why, she simply said that Desmond had an enormous capacity for love and it would be fitting for her to recognise that.

"Carol is not long for this earth and she is already being well catered for," Vincent protested.

"It doesn't matter. If Desmond chose this care facility he knew it to be worthy, and let's be honest, my daughter and granddaughter need nothing. It's something small that I can do in memory of the man I love," said Kes.

"You mean *loved*," Vincent corrected.

"No, I mean *love*," said the ever-stoic Kes.

Later that same week, Kes, Lauren and Eileen moved into the beautiful house that Desmond himself had designed and had builders and landscapers construct. The fresh sea air blowing in off the bays seemed to lift their spirits and Lauren savoured the new level of closeness with her mother.

A fortnight later, Kes passed away in her sleep. It was as if she knew her end was nigh. On top of her dresser drawers, she left a note which simply read:

For my daughter, Lauren, and granddaughter, Eileen – please treasure this for all your lives and Eileen, keep it for when you have children and grandchildren of your own. Cherish it always, as I have always cherished it.

Beneath the note was the red-covered book of prose by Desmond Jamieson.

Acknowledgements

When I embarked upon writing my first novel, this manuscript is not where I started.

Contact from a former work colleague, Graeme, whom I had not spoken to for the best part of twenty years, changed my direction completely.

Graeme had been trying to track me down for three or four years, to tell me that a very close and dear mutual friend had passed away five years earlier. That friend died of pancreatic cancer far too early and my recollection of her was one of vibrancy and passion for life.

As a result, I put my first and partly written manuscript aside to work on this novel instead. Many things change in one's lifetime, so this book has been a long time coming.

I have to thank my wife Lesley who has not only supported me in the best of times, but also most certainly, the lowest points of my life. Lesley deserves my eternal gratitude for her encouragement, along with my undying love.

Lesley also introduced me to my editor, Karen Crombie. Karen has given guidance and suggestions along the way but also the encouragement to keep going, for which I am immensely grateful.

There are many friends and loved ones that have supported and encouraged me in this endeavour; too many to mention, but they also have my gratitude.

I can only hope you enjoy the read and the journey.

Wayne